Murder in the Library

LOTTIE SPRIGG COUNTRY HOUSE MYSTERY BOOK 1

MARTHA BOND

ISBN 978-1-7396766-9-8

marthabond.com

Lottie Sprigg Country House Mystery Series

* * *

Murder in the Library
Murder in the Grotto

Chapter One

'BACK FROM FISHING ALREADY, TIMOTHY?' remarked Lady Abercromby as her husband sank into a chair beneath a portrait of his great-great-grandfather.

'Yes. Well observed of you, dear. I barely caught a thing today.'

'Oh dear, why's that?'

'I don't know, they must have been hiding. I landed a few salmon and some barbel. But not a single trout.'

'Maybe there are none left?' said Percy Abercromby, looking up from his book. 'Perhaps you've caught them all, Father?'

'Foolish boy! Of course I haven't caught them all. You could do with learning a thing or two about fishing. Your refusal to enjoy outdoor pursuits concerns me greatly. We can't have a future Lord Abercromby who doesn't know how to hunt, shoot and fish!'

'I prefer books, Father.'

'I know you prefer books, Percy. There's no need to remind me. Where's the tea got to?'

'It's not five yet, dear,' said Lady Abercromby. 'You're back early, remember?'

'And they can't bring tea earlier than five o'clock?'

'We could ask them, but I think it would make the new maid rather flustered.'

'Why? She's a maid. It's her job!'

'I realise that, Timothy, but let's keep to our usual routine until she's learned the ropes. I realise you're in a bad temper because the fishing didn't go well, but please don't take it out on the servants.'

'The trouble with fishing is that it's boring,' said Lord Abercromby. 'I'd much rather be galloping across fields with baying hounds or shooting things out of the sky. With fishing, one just simply sits there and waits.'

'It's good for your patience.'

'I don't have any patience, Elizabeth! And nor do I want any. Bring on the Glorious Twelfth when I can get at those grouse with my shotgun.' He turned to his son. 'And you're coming with me, Percy.'

'But I hate shooting things, Father!'

'You'll get accustomed to it soon enough. It's the sport of kings!'

'Hunting is the sport of kings, Timothy.'

'And I say shooting is too.'

Lady Abercromby sighed and returned to her needlework. Her husband was descended from a long line of stubborn Abercrombys and had firm ideas about how his heir should conduct himself. She'd explained to him that times were changing and every aristocratic family was having to adapt and alter its expectations of the younger generations. Timothy had pretended not to listen to her, but she hoped the idea was sinking in.

'Now, what do we have planned for this weekend?' said Lord Abercromby. 'Oh bother, I've just remembered. We've been invited to Fortescue Manor, haven't we? And it's the *very last thing* I want to do! I'd rather have my teeth pulled out with a giant pair of rusty pliers. Why on earth did you accept the invitation, Elizabeth?'

Lady Abercromby sighed. 'We've discussed this at great length, haven't we? We've decided the ancient feud between the Buckley-Phipps and the Abercromby families needs to end.'

'No member of the Abercromby family has set foot in Fortescue Manor since the Civil War!'

'So you have said many times. The Civil War was almost three hundred years ago. It's 1923 now, and I think we can be modern and grown up about these things, don't you? It's important to get on with one's neighbours.'

'I won't be able to get through the dinner without mentioning the boundary wall.'

'We don't need to go over this again, Timothy. Remember the rules we agreed upon? No mention of that wall. Don't forget it sent your grandfather to an early grave.'

'How can I forget? The Abercrombys have been wronged by that family for centuries! Ever since Lord Charles Buckley-Phipps stole thirty acres of our land when he built his wall.'

'In the middle of the seventeenth century, Timothy. Can't we agree to let the matter rest?'

'My father didn't.'

'No, he didn't. And look where it got him.'

'What do you mean by that?'

'He died a bitter old man, filled with anger.'

'Because of our neighbours!' He jabbed a finger in the general direction of Fortescue Manor. 'Lord Charles stole land which had been gifted to the Abercrombys by William the Conqueror. It's even recorded in the Domesday Book.'

'I've told you before to stop mentioning that book to me, Timothy.'

'It's an extremely important land survey!'

'From the *eleventh century*. I think we could all do with forgetting about it now. When we dine at Fortescue Manor, I want no mention of the wall or that book. Do you hear me, Timothy?'

'But Elizabeth!'

'Timothy!' She used a sharp tone, which made her husband's shoulders slump in defeat.

'Alright then.'

Lady Abercromby didn't share her husband's resentment of the Buckley-Phipps family. She'd felt touched by the invitation and saw it as the perfect opportunity to heal old wounds. As the country recovered after a dreadful war, it seemed petty to be arguing with one's neighbours over ancient disputes. 'It's time the Abercromby family turned over a new leaf,' she said. 'We're going to set an example to Percy and Evelyn.'

'You're still insisting on dragging them along, then?'

'Of course. They're our two eldest children and it's important they forge a friendship with the Buckley-Phipps family.'

'I'm looking forward to it,' said Percy, lifting his head from his book.

Lord Abercromby groaned. 'I never thought I'd see the day when I'd be visiting Fortescue Manor. It's enough to make my father turn in his grave!'

'HAMBLEDON HILL,' said Barty Buckley-Phipps as the motor car struggled up the steep gradient. 'We're nearly home!'

Lottie felt a fizz of excitement in her stomach. The last time she had been at Fortescue Manor, she'd been a maid. Now, after months abroad, she was returning as a travelling companion to Lady Buckley-Phipps' sister, Roberta Moore.

'Is the motor going to make it up the hill?' asked Mrs Moore. They were travelling no faster than walking pace.

'It's all your luggage, Auntie,' said Barty, turning round from the front passenger seat. 'It's weighing us down.'

'Most of my luggage is in the van behind us.'

'Then perhaps it's—'

'Don't you dare say it's me! You cheeky young man. I know what you're thinking.'

'I wouldn't dream of it, Auntie.'

Rosie, a Pembroke Welsh Corgi, sat on Lottie's lap and looked out of the window. Lottie had adopted Rosie in Venice, and this was the dog's first trip to England. 'I hope

5

Rosie is alright with the Dowager Lady Buckley-Phipps' dogs,' said Lottie. 'They can be quite noisy, can't they?'

'They certainly can,' said Mrs Moore. 'But their bite is worse than their bark.'

'You mean the other way round, Auntie,' said Barty.

'Do I? What did I say?'

Lottie smiled as the pair discussed the phrase and the car reached the brow of the hill. It picked up speed as it followed the lane down into the valley where Fortescue Manor nestled between the rolling Shropshire hills. The house's cream walls gleamed in the late afternoon sunshine. Before her travels with Mrs Moore, Lottie had worked at the house for five years. It was the closest place she had to home.

The car slowed as they approached a pair of grand gates, then turned into the long driveway which ran through the deer park.

'Home, sweet home!' said Barty. 'It feels a lifetime since I was here.'

'How is that possible?' said Mrs Moore. 'You've only been away for two weeks.'

Barty was the oldest of the Buckley-Phipps children. He'd been expelled from Oxford University in disgrace and sent to his aunt in Vienna as a punishment. Mrs Moore had visited Vienna hoping to secure her fourth marriage. But the arrangements had fallen through and they had returned to England sooner than expected.

Mrs Moore picked up her lorgnette and peered out at the deer park. 'The place is looking as beautiful as ever. Just think, Barty. One day, all this will be yours.'

'I'm not looking forward to all the work it will involve,' he said. 'I think I shall have to marry a lady who's happy to manage it all.'

'Oh Barty! You can't keep shirking responsibility. You're

twenty-one years old now. It's time to behave like a proper heir.'

'Where's the fun in that?'

'It's not supposed to be fun. It's your duty. You were born into it.'

'It's awfully unfair having no choice in the matter. Some days I wish I'd been born into a plain old ordinary family and didn't have to inherit a country pile and all the headaches that come with it.'

'Nonsense, Barty. You're an extremely privileged young man.'

'What do you think about it, Lottie?' he said. 'Would you rather grow up in an orphanage, free of family burdens, or inherit an estate?'

'I couldn't possibly say. I grew up in an orphanage, so it's the only life I know.'

'But you're happy, though?'

'Yes, I think so.'

'There you go, Auntie. I'd be much happier as an orphan too. I swear it!'

'Oh Barty, how ridiculous. Look, here's our welcoming party!'

The staff of Fortescue Manor stood in a neat line by the entrance to the house. As the car drew up, Lord and Lady Buckley-Phipps stepped out of the main entrance.

Two footmen in black suits and stiff white shirts stepped up to the car and opened the doors. Lottie felt her face heat with embarrassment. She still felt like a maid rather than a visiting dignitary. She stepped out onto the gravelled driveway with Rosie by her side. Mrs Moore stepped ahead of her to greet her sister. 'Lucinda!'

'Roberta!'

The two women embraced. They were similar in appearance, although Lady Buckley-Phipps was younger and a little slimmer.

'Barty,' said Lord Buckley-Phipps in a stern voice. He was a thick-set man with a double chin and sparkly green eyes. 'You were supposed to spend some time away learning your lesson.'

'I did, Father. I was away for two weeks.'

'I had six months in mind.'

'But two weeks is quite long enough. I learned my lesson quickly. I'm a changed young man. Just you wait and see.'

Lady Buckley-Phipps turned to Lottie. 'Look at you! You're quite grown up now. Your travels have transformed you from a girl into a fine young lady. Did you enjoy yourself?'

'Yes, my lady, it was quite an adventure.'

'I can't wait to hear more about your travels. And who's your delightful friend?'

'This is Rosie. We adopted her in Venice.'

Rosie wagged her tail and Lady Buckley-Phipps patted her on the head. 'What a lovely dog.'

The peace was interrupted by three Jack Russell dogs dashing over and barking excitedly.

'Don't worry, Rosie,' Lottie reassured her. 'They're very noisy, but they won't harm you.'

The corgi sat cowed as the three small dogs surrounded her and yapped. The Dowager Lady Buckley-Phipps stepped out of the house. She wore a lace-trimmed burgundy dress and carried an ornate walking stick.

'Wordsworth!' she shouted. 'That's quite enough! Come here! And you too, Shelley! Lord Byron!'

The dogs ignored her and continued to bark at Rosie.

The dowager pulled a whistle out of her handbag and gave it a sharp blow. Immediately, the dogs stopped their noise and ran back to her. They were rewarded for their trouble with some treats from the dowager's handbag.

Rosie's ears lifted, and she looked up at Lottie for reassurance. 'You'll be alright with them,' she said to her dog. 'Just let them be in charge and they'll be nice to you.'

'Let's go into the house, shall we?' said Lady Buckley-Phipps.

'I'm pleased you got my letter, Lucinda,' said Mrs Moore. 'I was worried you wouldn't be prepared for our return.'

'I was a little surprised when I received it, I thought you'd be away for longer.'

'So did I. In fact, I thought I would get married and live in a Bavarian castle. But it transpired the object of my affections, Prince Manfred of Bavaria, wasn't quite the man I had hoped he'd be. So we thought it would be best to return to Fortescue Manor.'

Lady Buckley-Phipps gave a sigh. 'I suppose you couldn't have known what was happening here.'

'Is something amiss?'

'I'd say so. In fact, you couldn't have chosen a worse time to come back.'

Chapter Three

'THE COOK HAS LEFT,' said Lady Buckley-Phipps as they made themselves comfortable in the sitting room.

'Mrs Evans?' said Mrs Moore. 'She's left, and that's why you're having a terrible time?'

'Yes. She's gone to work in the new biscuit factory in Oswestry. Apparently she'll be paid twice the salary there for half the work.'

'Golly. That sounds rather lucrative.'

'And that's not the end of it. The kitchen maid went with her. Can you believe it? And now we're short of staff while we try to find replacements. It's not proving easy! Gone are the days when servants worked for the love of their job rather than money. And it's difficult to recruit maids these days because young women would rather work in new factories or train at secretarial college. So the servants are having to fill the roles between them. Mrs Hudson, the housekeeper, is having to do some of the cook's work along with Mildred, one of the maids.'

A young maid, who Lottie didn't recognise, wheeled in

the trolley with afternoon tea on it. There was a large silver teapot, bone china mugs and plates of delicious looking cakes and scones.

'Thank you, Tilly,' said Lady Buckley-Phipps. 'No need to serve it out. You go and help Mrs Hudson and we can serve ourselves.' She got to her feet and walked over to the trolley. 'As you can see, I'm having to resort to a few chores myself.'

'There's nothing wrong with that, Lucinda.'

'Everything is wrong with it! It's not the life I'm accustomed to.'

'Perhaps it wouldn't hurt to do a few more things yourself? It would lower your weekly wage bill.'

'But I don't have time! I'm supposed to be running the household, not mucking in with chores! It's demeaning.' She began pouring out the tea.

'It's not demeaning, Lucinda. The world is changing. People are realising they don't have to go into service and there are other jobs they can do instead. Easier jobs which are better paid.'

'And what are people like us supposed to do?'

'Adapt.'

'But you've seen the size of this place, Roberta! How can we possibly run it with fewer staff? And to think I used my inheritance to rebuild it when the Buckley-Phipps were facing financial ruin. All that hard work and money. And for what? I can't bear the thought of it all crumbling around our ears again.'

'I'm sure things won't get that bad, Lucinda. I'm happy to help with whatever needs doing while I'm here. In fact, I enjoyed being self-sufficient during our travels. Lottie and I did lots of things for ourselves, we certainly weren't waited on hand and foot.'

'That's because you only had yourselves to think about.'

11

'And very refreshing it was, too. I can recommend it. In fact, why don't you and Ivan do something similar?'

'You're forgetting I have twelve children, Roberta.'

'The eldest, Barty, is an adult. And the older ones are at boarding school.'

'But they come home for holidays.'

'The governesses, nannies and nursery nurses keep an eye on them as well as take care of the younger ones.'

'I still devote some time each day to my motherly duties. I don't think you understand the demands of being a mother, Roberta.' She handed a cup of tea to her husband.

'Good grief. Who made this?' he said. 'It's the colour of—'

'Careful, Ivan. We don't want any rude words,' said Lady Buckley-Phipps.

'What makes you think I was going to say rude words?'

'Because we can all see the colour of the tea. Several unsavoury comparisons come to mind. However, Tilly has only been with us a short while. She's still learning how to make tea.'

'It's terrible it really is, I've never known anything like it,' said Lord Buckley-Phipps. 'Gone are the days when local people were grateful to be working in a place like this. In my father's day, it was an honour. Generations of local families served generations of my family. And now it's all changing! The new biscuit factory hasn't helped matters at all. Not only do they have shorter hours there and good pay, but the workers are allowed to take home boxes of broken biscuits! We can't compete. And now you can't even find someone who can make a decent pot of tea.'

'Lottie always used to make excellent tea,' said Lady Buckley-Phipps.

'Don't get any ideas, Lucinda,' said Mrs Moore. 'She's employed as my travelling companion now. Her days of working here as a maid are behind her.'

Lottie felt happy Mrs Moore had swiftly leapt to her defence. With Fortescue Manor being under-staffed, she was worried she might be called upon to carry out maid duties again.

Chapter Four

THE DOWAGER LADY Buckley-Phipps entered the room, tapping her walking stick on the floor. Her three dogs trotted over to Rosie and yapped at her. The corgi's ears flopped and her eyes grew wide and doleful.

'Keep your nose to yourself, Lord Byron,' said the dowager. She sank into an easy chair and her dogs returned to her and sat by her feet.

'Mother, I really must speak with you about your pets,' said Lord Buckley-Phipps. 'I went to put on my favourite pair of Wellington boots this morning and discovered that an animal had chewed through the toe of one of them.'

'How do you know it was an animal?'

'Because I don't think a person would have done it.'

'Perhaps it was a rat?'

'If a rat has jaws that size, then we have a serious pest problem. It can only have been one of your dogs. I know they like to chew things and I've told you before not to let them into the boot room.'

'I didn't let them in there, Ivan. Someone must have left the door open.'

'I shall have a word with the servants about that. But please make sure you keep your dogs with you, Mother. They can do untold damage when they're left unsupervised, and I can no longer wear my favourite pair of Wellington boots.'

'You can borrow my Wellington boots, Father,' said Barty.

'Not likely, they're too fashionable. I don't want to look like a dandy.'

'A dandy? They're just normal Wellington boots.'

'Barty, what's happened with your disgrace?' asked the dowager.

'Hopefully it's come to an end, Granny.'

'Already?'

'Yes. I've told Father that I'm a changed young man.'

'It's not me you need to persuade,' said Lord Buckley-Phipps. 'It's Oxford University.'

'I intend to go back in September and tell them it was a misunderstanding. I shall explain to the college dean exactly what happened with his daughter, Florence. It was completely innocent.'

'Haven't you already explained it to him?'

'Yes, but he was angry at the time and didn't listen. Hopefully, he'll have calmed down now and will hear me out. All we'd intended was a nice picnic while punting, but then I lost the oar in some duckweed and we were set adrift on the River Cherwell. It could have happened to anyone.'

'I don't see why you had to be out all night.'

'Because we were out in the sticks, Father. There was no one else about! Apart from the generous farmworker who returned us to Oxford by tractor at sunrise the following morning. Florence will back up my story. In fact, with a bit of luck, the dean has listened to her now and finally believes us. Maybe I'll be able to waltz back into Oxford with no one blinking an eye.'

'You sound confident about it, Barty, so you'd better be

right. If you fail to get back into Oxford, then I'll have no choice but to send you to Sandhurst.'

'Oh no, Father, not the army!'

'Sandhurst never did me any harm.'

'I can't bear all that shouting they do in the army. And I'd be completely hopeless with a gun. In fact, I'd be dangerous.'

'I don't disagree with you there. So it's important you get back into Oxford.'

'Ivan, have you told Barty yet about the Abercrombys coming to dinner?' said the dowager.

'Lord and Lady Abercromby?' said Barty. 'Coming here for dinner? But they're our avowed foe!'

'Your mother disagrees,' said Lord Buckley-Phipps. 'She has extended an olive branch to them.'

'I certainly have,' said Lady Buckley-Phipps.

Lottie felt surprised by this news. During the time she'd worked at Fortescue Manor, there had been nothing but scorn for the Abercromby family in the neighbouring estate, Clarendon Park.

'We've decided that, after centuries of arguing, the two families should make an effort to get along with each other,' said Lady Buckley-Phipps. 'At times like this, noble families need to stick together. The Abercrombys must also be losing their staff to the Oswestry biscuit factory. I would like to find out how they're managing.'

'You and Lady Abercromby have made your minds up about this,' said Lord Buckley-Phipps. 'But I suspect Lord Abercromby is as appalled by the prospect as I am.'

'It would never have happened in your father's day, Ivan,' said the Dowager Lady Buckley-Phipps. 'But I suppose times change.'

'Remind me why there was a fallout,' said Mrs Moore. 'I'm sure you explained it to me once, Lucinda, but I've forgotten.'

'Just after the Civil War, Lord Charles Buckley-Phipps decided to put a wall around this estate,' said Lord Buckley-Phipps. 'And Lord Abercromby objected to it.'

'Why?'

'He said Lord Charles had stolen thirty acres of his land.'

'And had he?'

'No,' said the dowager. 'And besides, the Abercromby estate is over twenty thousand acres. What's a mere thirty acres between friends?'

Thirty acres seemed a lot to Lottie. She knew one acre wasn't much smaller than a football pitch.

'Thirty acres is still stealing,' said Mrs Moore.

The dowager's lips pursed. 'My late husband's great-great-great-great-grandfather never stole from anyone! That wall boundary was perfectly legal. The maps which the Abercromby family possessed were out of date!'

Lady Buckley-Phipps sighed. 'This is an argument which has dragged on for nearly three hundred years. That's why Lady Abercromby and I have decided to make peace with it. The Abercrombys are dining with us this weekend and everyone has to promise they'll be on their best behaviour so we can all have a lovely time.'

'I know my father would never have agreed to this, but times are changing, I suppose,' said Lord Buckley-Phipps.

'I think it's an excellent idea, Lucinda,' said Mrs Moore. 'Life is too short to be falling out with people.'

'It's also too short to suffer fools,' said Lord Buckley-Phipps.

'I think you'll be pleasantly surprised, Ivan,' said Lady Buckley-Phipps. 'Percy and Evelyn Abercromby will also be joining us.'

'Oh no, not Percy!' said Barty. 'We were at school together. He's such a frightful telltale.'

'That was a few years ago,' said Lady Buckley-Phipps. 'I'm

17

sure he's quite changed now. He's twenty-one, like you, Barty, and is doing well at Cambridge.'

'Indeed,' said Lord Buckley-Phipps. 'He's managed to study there for two years without being kicked out.'

'That's because he's a bore and a swot.'

'Barty! That's enough!' said Lady Buckley-Phipps.

'Barty's not wrong,' said Lord Buckley-Phipps. 'There's no doubt that young Percy is wet behind the ears.'

'Why don't we reserve judgement on everyone until we spend time with them?' said Lady Buckley-Phipps. 'We're talking about events which happened in the past. Everyone is probably quite changed these days.'

'Excellent dear, that's what we'll do,' said her husband. 'We'll reserve judgement and then I shall enjoy watching you resisting the urge to tear the hair out of your head before we've even got to the fish course.'

Chapter Five

'I'm staying in the Rose Suite, Lottie,' said Mrs Moore as they made their way up the grand staircase after tea. 'And Lady Buckley-Phipps says you can have the delightful little room next to it.'

'Oh.' Lottie was disappointed to hear it. 'I just assumed I would be in my old room.'

'In the attics?'

'Yes.'

'But the room next to the Rose Suite is much more comfortable.'

'Perhaps it is. But I like my old room. Unless...' Lottie stopped on the staircase. 'I suppose someone else may be in it now.'

'I doubt it. This place has far more servant bedrooms than it needs these days. If you're really sure you'll be happy in your old room, then I'm sure my sister won't object.'

A short while later, Lottie climbed the narrow wooden staircase with Rosie in tow. The ceiling was low in the attics and there was no carpet on the floorboards, but Lottie felt happy to be back here. She pushed open the door of her room and was delighted to find it just as she'd left it. There was an iron bedstead against one wall, a wardrobe against the other, and a colourful rug on the floor. The shelf above the bed still had all her books on it.

What Lottie loved most about her room was the view from the little window. From here, she had a view over the lake with its elegant weeping willows. Beyond the lake, emerald green fields rose up to Hambledon Hill. Out of sight, behind the hill, lay the village of Lowton Chorley.

She turned to Rosie. 'It feels nice to be back. I'm sure you'll enjoy it here. We can go for long walks in the gardens.'

A knock at the door interrupted her.

'Come in!' she called out and a young woman with red hair, freckles, chubby cheeks and chubby arms stepped in.

'Mildred!' said Lottie. She embraced her old friend.

'I thought you were going to be staying downstairs,' said Mildred. 'With all the ladies and gentlemen.'

'No, I wanted to be back in my old room.'

Mildred grinned. 'I've kept it dusted for you.'

'Thank you!'

'And you've got a dog.'

'Yes, this is Rosie.'

The corgi sniffed at Mildred's apron and she patted her on the head.

Lottie suspected Mildred didn't know how to act with her now that she was no longer a maid. 'It's lovely to see you again, Mildred.'

'You've changed a lot!' said the maid. 'Look at your fancy clothes!'

'Fancy?' Lottie glanced down at her blouse, jacket and skirt. 'They're nothing special. But I suppose we did buy them in Paris.'

Mildred clapped her hands to her face. 'Paris! I can't even imagine what it must be like being somewhere like that.'

'It's a lovely city, I'm sure you'll visit one day.'

'I don't see how.'

'I thought that once, too. But you never know.'

'So where did you go?'

'Paris, Venice, Monaco, Vienna and Cairo.'

'Cairo? That's in Egypt, isn't it?'

Lottie nodded.

'Did you see the pyramids?'

'Yes.'

'I think I'd faint with excitement if I saw the pyramids in real life!'

'I'm sure you'd be fine. Hopefully you'll get to go there as well one day.'

'I doubt it.' Mildred wiped her hands on her apron and glanced at the bare mattress on the bed. 'I'll fetch some bed linen and I'll get that made up.'

When Mildred returned with the sheets, Lottie helped make the bed. 'How have things been here?' she asked.

'Same as always. Although we lost Mrs Evans, she's working in the biscuit factory now. Along with Ethel. She's gone too. And they can't get replacements, so me and Mrs Hudson have been doing the cooking.'

'That can't be easy. You must be very busy. I heard Lady Buckley-Phipps mention Mrs Evans left, she's quite upset about it.'

'Cook said she wasn't getting any younger and couldn't do the hours anymore. And the new biscuit factory is a good place to work. The managers are friendly, there's lots of breaks and you get free biscuits.'

'I think Lady Buckley-Phipps is worried she's losing her staff.'

'That's not surprising, there are more jobs about now. I

21

can see why people want to work in a factory. It beats working twelve hours a day with only one afternoon off every fortnight.'

'I remember it well,' said Lottie with a sigh. She felt lucky she didn't have to do a maid's job anymore. But she felt guilty too. Mildred was still doing the same old chores while and Lottie had nice clothes, a kind employer, and an opportunity to travel. 'It's not fair,' she said.

'Why isn't it fair?'

'Because I no longer have to do what you do. For some reason, Mrs Moore chose me to accompany her rather than someone else. You could easily do my job, Mildred.'

'One of the reasons she chose you was because you speak French. She knew that would come in useful on her travels. And also because you're clever and are someone who can be trusted.'

'That's very kind of you to say so, Mildred. But that doesn't make me any better than you or anyone else who works here. I suppose speaking French is useful. And I only know it because they taught us in the orphanage.'

'You deserve the job you have now, Lottie.' Mildred smiled. 'You were always cleverer than me and don't deny it. I need to get back to the kitchen to help Mrs Hudson. Do you want to come and say hello to everyone?'

'Yes I would.'

Chapter Six

LOTTIE FELT nervous as she descended the staircase to the basement.

'Come on!' said Mildred, noticing her hesitancy. 'Everyone will be pleased to see you.'

In the past, Lottie had used these stairs countless times each day. But after a few months away, the memories seemed long ago. She felt she didn't belong here anymore.

She heard the buzz of voices as they approached the servants' hall. Rosie trotted happily by her side.

'Here she is!' said Mildred, marching into the room. Lottie lingered bashfully behind her, wishing Mildred hadn't announced her presence so obviously.

Mrs Hudson, the housekeeper, was the first to greet her. 'Miss Sprigg,' she said. 'How nice it is to see you again.' The housekeeper had never addressed Lottie by her surname before. It was going to take some time to get used to it.

'It's nice to see you too, Mrs Hudson.' Lottie wasn't sure how true this really was. The housekeeper was an intimidating figure with her stern expression and long, dark dress. But Mrs Hudson gave her a slight smile and Lottie wondered if there was another side to the housekeeper which she might see more of from now on.

Mr Duxbury, the butler, acknowledged her with a formal nod. He was a broad-shouldered, bald man with a prominent nose. 'I trust you enjoyed your travels, Miss Sprigg?'

'I did. Thank you, Mr Duxbury.'

'And you found a new companion?' he said, smiling at Rosie. Mr Duxbury didn't smile very often and the corgi was happy to greet him with her tail wagging.

'Yes, her name's Rosie,' said Lottie. 'I adopted her in Venice.'

'Venice?' said Harry, the footman. 'Very fancy.'

'Come and have a cup of tea,' said Mildred, pulling out a chair for Lottie. 'And you can tell everyone all about it.'

'I don't want to bore people,' said Lottie, taking a seat. She felt a little embarrassed by the attention.

'Lottie's seen the pyramids!' Mildred announced to everyone.

'The pyramids?' said Mr Duxbury. 'How spectacular. Did you see the Sphinx too?'

'Yes, I did.'

'I would love to see the Sphinx,' he said, taking a sip of tea. 'I fancy it will be something I do in retirement, but I'll probably be too old and frail by then.'

'Oh nonsense, Mr Duxbury,' said Mrs Hudson. 'You're as fit as a fiddle still.'

'Still?' He paused with his cup below his chin.

'I mean now. You're as fit as a fiddle now. And I'm quite sure you'll remain so.'

'Did you go on one of those boats in Venice?' asked the new maid.

'You mean a gondola, Tilly,' said Mrs Hudson.

'Yeah. One of those.'

'Yes I did,' said Lottie. She was tempted to include the

amusing story of Mrs Moore falling into a canal, but decided against it. She answered a few more questions about her travels before Mr Duxbury announced the tea break was over.

'It's lovely to see you all again,' Lottie said to everyone.

'Now you can go back upstairs, Miss Sprigg, and mingle with the respectable people,' said Harry, the footman. There was a coldness in his eyes as he spoke.

Lottie suspected he was envious of her new position, but his hostility made her feel uncomfortable.

Chapter Seven

AFTER BREAKFAST THE FOLLOWING MORNING, Lottie, Rosie and Mrs Moore took a walk around the lake. The sun was already high in the sky and a fresh, warm breeze blew through the valley, rustling the leaves on the weeping willow trees.

'What a lovely morning,' said Mrs Moore. She surveyed their surroundings through her lorgnette. 'I'd forgotten how beautiful it is here. So green! That's the benefit of all the rain they get here I suppose. How do you feel about being back at Fortescue Manor, Lottie?'

'I'm happy to be back because this place feels like home to me. But it also feels a little strange because I'm no longer one of the maids. When I woke up this morning, I almost got up to get started on the day's chores! I feel guilty that Mildred is still doing that job. It's hard work.'

'I can understand why you feel guilty, but you must remember why you're no longer a maid, Lottie. It's because you have the ability to do much more. I don't mean that disrespectfully towards Mildred, but you have always been a clever girl and you're in the position you are now because you earned it. Oh dear, I make it sound as though my travelling companion is a prestigious role. It isn't really, is it?' She laughed.

'It's more prestigious than being a maid. Luckily, Mildred doesn't seem to begrudge me for that.'

'If she's a proper friend, then she won't. Only an untrustworthy friend would become jealous about such things. That's how you know you have a good friendship.'

Rosie scampered after a dove which had settled nearby. It rose up into the air again long before she could reach it.

'How long do you think we'll stay here for?' Lottie asked Mrs Moore.

'That's a good question. I adore Fortescue Manor and my sister has said we can stay here for as long as we like. I feel the need for a rest after my disappointment in Vienna. I enjoyed our stay there, but it was difficult when I realised the dream I was pursuing was little more than... a dream. I can't think of a better way of putting it. It made me realise I need to have a better idea of what I want from life. I would like to marry again because I miss not having a husband. But I don't feel the same urgency as I did before. It's funny to think how fixated I became on Prince Manfred! What a fool I've been.'

'I don't think you've been a fool.'

'That's very kind of you to say so, Lottie. When my third husband left me, all I could think about was finding a fourth husband. Now I've realised I don't have to do that. I have you and Rosie for company now and I enjoy that. I also enjoy coming here and seeing my sister and her family, so I feel grateful for the people who are in my life. I'm happy now to wait for a marriage opportunity to come along rather than actively seek one out.'

'That makes sense. After all, there's no hurry.'

'That's a fine thing for you to say, Lottie, You're thirty years younger than me!' She laughed. 'But you're right, too. I think when we try to hurry things, we make mistakes, don't we? When we're rushing to make a decision, it can sometimes be poorly thought out. So I shall wait for opportunities to present themselves. In the meantime, we can enjoy the rest of this glorious summer in the beautiful Shropshire countryside. After that, it will be time to return to Chelsea. Oh look, who's this?' She raised her lorgnette and surveyed the lanky young man with a distinctive bouncing gait. 'It's Barty!'

Rosie ran up to him and greeted him.

'How are you this morning, Barty?' said Mrs Moore.

'Very nervous.' He took off his boater hat and pushed his fair hair out of his eyes.

'Why?'

'Because the Abercrombys are coming to dinner! I think it's a completely hare-brained idea. Our two families haven't seen eye-to-eye for centuries. I don't understand why Mother is bothered about making amends now.'

Although she'd worked at Fortescue Manor for five years, Lottie had never encountered anyone from the Abercromby family. She'd heard various members of the Buckley-Phipps family complain about them, though. She was looking forward to finding out what they were really like.

'Isn't it nicer to get along with your neighbours than argue with them, Barty?' said Mrs Moore.

'I don't know. Is it? The very last person I want to see is telltale tit Percy Abercromby. I'll never forget the time at school when I thought it would be enormous fun to put a rotten egg under the cushion on the Latin master's chair. Not only did Abercromby warn him not to sit down, but he also told him I was the one who put it there! He has no sense of fun whatsoever. I received a caning for that one.'

'I'm sure Percy isn't a telltale anymore,' said Mrs Moore.

'But what if he is? I shouldn't think he's changed much at all.'

'What's Evelyn Abercromby like?'

'The last time I saw her, she was about this high.' He held his hand at a level just above his knee. 'And she was snivelling.'

'She must be eighteen or nineteen years old now. I'm sure she's not doing that anymore.'

'Oh she will be, mark my words! Those Abercrombys never change!'

Chapter Eight

LOTTIE THOUGHT the Abercromby family seemed pleasant when they arrived for dinner that evening. Lady Abercromby was a tall, elegant lady dressed in a raspberry red gown with layered skirts. Jewels sparkled at her ears, wrists and throat. Her husband was lean and had a thick grey moustache. Long strands of grey hair were neatly oiled across his balding head.

'Thank you so much for the dinner invitation, Lady Buckley-Phipps,' said Lady Abercromby.

'It's my pleasure.' Lady Buckley-Phipps smiled warmly. Her evening dress was topaz blue with a Chinese pattern embroidered in gold. Her jewels sparkled almost as brightly as Lady Abercromby's. 'I thought it was about time our families sat together under the same roof,' she said. 'I can't believe it's not happened for almost three hundred years.'

'Yes. Quite astonishing, isn't it? And difficult to believe any of our ancestors refused to bury the hatchet.'

The dowager, as one of the ancestors, glared at Lady Abercromby but said nothing. She wore a jade green long-sleeved dress with a fitted bodice. Against her wishes, her dogs had been shut in the gunroom for the evening, so they couldn't bother the guests.

'Well, here's to a pleasant evening,' said Lord Abercromby, raising his glass of champagne.

'Yes, indeed!' added Lord Buckley-Phipps, clearly under instruction from his wife to be convivial. He raised his glass, then took a sip.

Barty stood at one side of the room, giving Percy Abercromby cautious side-glances. He clearly felt no wish to rekindle any association they'd had during their school days.

Percy was a lean young man who resembled his father, except his hair was thick and dark and his front teeth protruded so he couldn't close his mouth. Fortunately for Evelyn, she didn't look like her brother. Her hair was fair, like her mother's, and she wore a fashionable lemon-yellow dress and a beaded hairband. The three young people remained quiet as their parents discussed the safe topic of the weather.

Mrs Moore was dressed in a turquoise dress with layers of organza. Her outfit made her look twice the size of everyone else in the room, but Lottie knew she wouldn't mind that. Lottie's dress was mulberry satin, and Mrs Moore had persuaded her to wear one of her feather boas with it. It had intrigued Rosie, and she'd sniffed it so much that a little feather had stuck to her nose and made her sneeze.

Lottie remained quiet, sipping her champagne and feeling a little out of place. She also felt nervous. Some members of the Buckley-Phipps family had strong opinions about the Abercrombys, and she could only hope it would all go without a hitch.

At dinner, Lottie sat between the Dowager Lady Buckley-Phipps and Evelyn. Candlelight from tall candelabras sparkled in the crystal glasses and silverware. A display from the gardens of Fortescue Manor formed a table centrepiece, it contained some pretty peach-coloured roses which the dowager had probably cut. Lottie knew she liked to help maintain the rose garden in the summer months.

An array of cutlery was arranged in each place setting, Lottie tried to plan what she should use for each course. Rosie sat beneath the table, resting against Lottie's leg.

'So you're a travelling companion now, Miss Sprigg,' said the dowager. 'How does that compare to being a maid?'

'It's very different. But I'm enjoying it a lot.'

The dowager lowered her voice. 'Mrs Moore is quite unlucky in love, isn't she? How many times has she been married?'

'Three.'

'I don't understand how one gets through three husbands.' Lottie glanced across the table at her employer, who was chatting animatedly with Barty. She hoped Mrs Moore wouldn't be able to hear what the dowager was saying. 'One husband was enough for me,' said the dowager. 'And we were loyal to each other for over fifty years. I'm still loyal to him now, even though he's six feet under!' She gave a little laugh. 'That's a true marriage in my belief. I could never consider marrying again. Didn't Mrs Moore set her sights on a fourth husband and chase him across Europe?'

'She followed him rather than chased him.'

'Sounds like the same thing to me. Chasing after a man was something we never did in our day. It was considered most unladylike. But times have changed, I suppose. Young women these days are getting their hair cut so short they look like boys. And as for some of their dresses...' The old lady gave a shudder. 'They don't seem to care that people can see their legs. I don't know where it's all going to end.' She lowered her voice further still. 'And now we have to make friends with the Abercrombys. I think it must be because Lucinda is American. She doesn't understand the ancient customs we have here.'

'Such as falling out with neighbours?'

'I'm talking about the old families of these isles. We have a nature which is very peculiar to ourselves. I don't suppose you can expect an outsider to understand that.'

Lottie thought it odd the old lady considered her daughter-in-law as an outsider twenty-five years after she'd married into the Buckley-Phipps family. It probably explained why the pair didn't see eye-to-eye.

'I think the dinner this evening is a good idea,' said Lottie.

'Perhaps it is,' said the dowager, peering at the bowl of lobster bisque which had just been placed in front of her. 'Time will tell, I suppose. Although the Abercromby heir is an intriguing individual.' She glanced at Percy. He was politely answering questions posed by Lady Buckley-Phipps. 'You do realise he's the Abercromby's only boy? The rest of the children are girls. Imagine what would become of the Clarendon Park estate if something happened to him? It would probably go to a distant family member. At least Lucinda had the sense to have a few more sons after Barty. It does no harm to have some spares.'

Lord Buckley-Phipps sat at one end of the table and appeared to find plenty to laugh about with Lady Abercromby. So much so that Lady Buckley-Phipps and Lord Abercromby kept glancing at them from their end of the table.

Mr Duxbury the butler kept a keen eye on everything and Edward the footman served Dover sole for the fish course. Harry followed him with a silver sauce boat. The dowager spooned some brown butter sauce onto her fish. Lottie waited patiently, but Harry passed her by and offered the sauce to Evelyn on her left. Lottie felt sure he'd missed her deliberately. She chose not to mention it and instead spoke to Evelyn about horses. Lottie knew little about them, but she realised if she asked Evelyn a few questions, the young woman was happy to talk at length about the stables at Clarendon Park and the favourite horses she liked to ride.

As Evelyn talked, Lottie noticed Barty watching her. He probably wished he was sitting in Lottie's place rather than sandwiched between Mrs Moore and Percy.

'My dear, you haven't got any butter sauce!' said the dowager. 'I shall summon the footman!'

'Oh no, it's quite alright, thank you, my lady. I declined it.'

'Declined butter sauce?'

'Yes. I'm quite happy with my fish as it is. Thank you.'

'But sole is so dry without sauce!'

The dowager's comments were loud enough to be heard by the rest of the table. Mr Duxbury raised a concerned eyebrow and Lottie knew she could get Harry into trouble if she chose to mention he'd ignored her. She decided against it because she didn't want to cause a fuss.

'Don't forget Lottie was raised in an orphanage,' said Lady Buckley-Phipps. 'She's quite accustomed to plain food.'

'That's right,' said Lottie, embarrassed she was now receiving everyone's attention.

I hadn't thought of that,' said the dowager. 'Being raised in an orphanage must be a bleak experience. Do you ever wonder who your parents were, Miss Sprigg?'

'Mother!' said Lord Buckley-Phipps. 'I don't think Miss Sprigg would like to be reminded of upsetting things.'

'I don't mind at all, my lord,' said Lottie. 'And, in answer to your question, my lady, I do think about who my parents could have been quite a lot. I imagine my mother must have found herself in difficult circumstances and I can only hope she found a better life for herself in the end.'

'What a lovely sentiment, Lottie!' said Lady Abercromby. 'Just think how bitter and upset you could be about it and yet you don't blame your mother at all. That shows strong character.'

'Lottie certainly has strong character,' said Mrs Moore. 'Why else do you think I chose her as my travelling companion?'

'And my sister's gain was my loss,' said Lady Buckley-Phipps. Lottie felt flattered by this, but she also felt uncomfortable being discussed. Thankfully, Lady Buckley-Phipps changed the subject. 'I wonder, Lady Abercromby, if you've been experiencing the same problems we have with staff? We've lost quite a few to the biscuit factory in Oswestry.'

'Oh, that biscuit factory!' Lady Abercromby lay down her knife and fork. 'I swear it's stolen a third of our staff so far this year. Wouldn't you say, Timothy?'

'Yes, I'd say.'

'I really don't understand why a biscuit factory is more appealing than working in a country house. But it seems it is.'

'Double the pay and half the hours is what I've heard,' said Lady Buckley-Phipps.

'Is that so? Well, I don't know how we can compete with that. We don't have the budget to increase staff wages. Our running costs are quite extraordinary these days. I expect it's the same for you.'

'Yes, it is! There's always a part of the house threatening to fall down. Installing electricity was a large outlay, too.'

'The same for us!' said Lady Abercromby. 'And we made the mistake of using a dreadful electrician from Oswestry. For the first few months, we kept getting electric shocks whenever we turned on a light.'

'Bodbury?'

'Yes, that's the one! You used him and his men, too?'

'Yes! They did a terrible job, didn't they, Ivan?'

'Yes, they did.'

Coq au vin was served as the main course and Lottie passed a piece of chicken to Rosie beneath the table.

'You're lucky, Miss Sprigg,' said the dowager in a quiet voice. 'You're allowed to have your dog with you. My three have been shut in the gunroom while we eat.'

Lottie thought this was a good idea, but she tried to be sympathetic. 'I'm sorry to hear it.'

'Ivan insists on it, so I suppose I must do as he says. After all, it would be a disaster if one of them bit one of the guests, wouldn't it? That would ruin any chances of mending the three-hundred-year-old feud.'

Duck a l'orange was served as the game course. And once again, Harry the footman deliberately left Lottie out when he came round with the sauce. This time, she caught his eye, and the coldness of his stare made her shiver.

Chapter Nine

'How DID you enjoy your travels, Mrs Moore?' asked Lady Abercromby as everyone tucked into the game course.

'I enjoyed my travels enormously, my lady.'

'Where did you go?'

'Venice, Paris, Cairo, Monaco and Vienna.'

'Lovely. I've been to all of those places too. Aren't they delightful?'

'I wouldn't call Cairo delightful,' said Lord Abercromby.

'Oh it is, Timothy, it's only because the food disagreed with you.'

'It more than disagreed with me, Elizabeth. It almost killed me!'

'Now you're exaggerating, Timothy.'

'I am not! I spent over twelve hours stuck in the—'

'There's no need to share the details, Timothy, especially when everyone's eating.' Lady Abercromby addressed Mrs Moore again. 'Which was your favourite city?'

'It's quite impossible to say. Although I do have a soft spot for Monte Carlo.'

'Oh absolutely! Who doesn't? And am I right in thinking you went out there to find a husband?'

'There was a gentleman who I considered a suitable prospect for a while. But then I decided he was unsuitable.'

'How disappointing. Men are often quite disappointing, don't you find?'

'Excuse me, Elizabeth,' said Lord Abercromby. 'But you're forgetting there are four thoroughly decent gentlemen sitting at this table.' He gestured at the others with his fork. 'I ask that you kindly retract that statement.'

'I shan't retract it, but I shall say that present company is excluded from it.'

'Well, it's a rather sweeping statement, Elizabeth. And not a lot of truth in it, either.'

'I think Roberta is living proof that it's difficult to find the perfect gentleman to marry,' said Lady Buckley-Phipps. 'She's been married three times and has just ruled out a potential fourth. I suppose I was lucky meeting Ivan. But I can see why many women get fed up with trying to find the perfect husband.'

'I'm not fed up!' said Mrs Moore. 'I'm quite happy as I am. If I never married again, then I would be perfectly content. And besides, I much prefer being foot-loose and fancy-free to being burdened by a vast ancestral home. It must be like having an albatross hanging around your neck.'

'You cannot possibly compare Fortescue Manor to an albatross, Roberta! That just won't do!'

'What suits you doesn't suit me, Lucinda.'

'But don't you wish you'd married someone with a title, Mrs Moore?' asked Lady Abercromby.

'No. There was an opportunity at one time to marry into the Bavarian royal family, and that would have come with an extremely fancy title. But none of that impresses me now. If my travels taught me something, it's that you can have all the wealth and nobility in the world and still be a... actually I'll stop myself there. I don't want to say any rude words at the dinner table.'

'Well, that's told us,' said Lord Buckley-Phipps. 'What do you make of all this, Barty?'

'Me?'

'Yes.'

'Of what?'

'What we were just discussing. How important is wealth and nobility?'

'Erm... quite important, I suppose.'

'Do you not have a firmer opinion than that? Come on, young man, you're the heir! If you're to manage this estate properly, you need to have strong opinions about everything!'

'Do I?'

Lord Abercromby chuckled. 'We have just the same problem with Percy, Lord Buckley-Phipps. As each year passes, I attempt to involve him more in the management of Clarendon Park, but he'd much rather read books about ancient battles.'

'Because that's what I'm interested in, Father,' said Percy.

'And you also need to be interested in the family estate. How on earth is it going to be managed after I'm dead and gone?'

'I'll marry someone who knows what she's doing, Father,' said Percy. 'Just as you did. I remember Granny telling me she and Grandfather had no hope at all in your—'

'Hold your tongue, Percy,' snapped his mother. 'Do not speak about your father in that way. And especially in polite company. It's most rude.'

Lord Abercromby smiled at Lord Buckley-Phipps. 'It seems we're both faced with a common problem,' he said. 'A recalcitrant heir. I blame the modern world. There are too many distractions for young men these days and all sense of family loyalty has gone.'

'I couldn't agree more,' said Lord Buckley-Phipps. He turned to Percy. 'So you like reading about old battles, do you?' he asked.

'Oh yes, I enjoy them enormously.'

'May I ask why?'

'Because it's interesting to learn about the various strategies which were used. What worked and what didn't work and why. The Battle of Winchelsea was an interesting one because—'

'Not now, Percy,' said his father.

'But I was only going to explain about—'

'I'm sure you were. But we don't want to bore our hosts with historical lectures. It's impolite and is something the ladies certainly won't be interested in.'

'No we're not,' said Evelyn. 'I don't understand why you find boring old battles so interesting, Percy.'

'They formed the history of our lands!'

'But that doesn't make them interesting. Those battles must have been horrible, just think of all the people who were killed and injured! In fact, I don't like to think about it. It's upsetting.'

'I agree with you, Evelyn,' said her mother. 'But Percy is allowed to have his interests. Just as you have yours.'

'What are your interests, Miss Abercromby?' asked Mrs Moore.

'Horses,' she replied. 'Proper living beings with personality. I love being around them.'

'How lovely,' said Mrs Moore. 'I can't say I get on with them well myself, but I can certainly see the attraction.'

'I like horses,' said Barty, smiling at Evelyn.

'Do you ride?' she asked him.

'I try to. I'm not very good at it though.'

'Perhaps I could help you improve?' she said.

Barty's eyes widened, as if he couldn't believe what she'd just said. 'Help me? Oh. Goodness. Perhaps. Yes.'

Lottie smiled. She had never seen Barty tongue-tied before.

'You might like to have a browse in our library after dinner, Mr Abercromby,' said Lord Buckley-Phipps. 'We have a ten-volume series on the English Civil War. Barty will show you it.'

'Will I?' said Barty.

'Yes, you will. It's a series of books which belonged to your grandfather and he took a great interest in them. I'm sure he'd be delighted if Mr Abercromby also took an interest in them. I can't say they're at risk of being read by anyone in this household.'

'Thank you Lord Buckley-Phipps,' said Lord Abercromby. 'But I fear you're merely encouraging my son in his solitary pursuits.'

'If he has interests, then they should be encouraged! As long as you agree to also listen to your father about the running of Clarendon Park, Mr Abercromby.'

'I do listen,' said Percy.

'Good.'

'Well, I think it's an excellent idea that Barty shows Percy the books in the library,' said Lady Buckley-Phipps. 'It's a wonderful opportunity for the two heirs to get along with one another.'

'I agree,' said Lord Abercromby. 'And while we're on the topic of getting along, I'd like to say a few words, if I may.'

'Really, Father?' said Evelyn.

'Quiet,' hissed her mother.

'Go ahead!' said Lord Buckley-Phipps.

Lord Abercromby picked up his wine glass and got to his feet. 'I must admit that when I first received the invitation to dine here at Fortescue Manor with Lord and Lady Buckley-Phipps, I was all prepared to throw it into the fire.'

'Oh,' said Lady Buckley-Phipps. 'That isn't very nice to hear.'

'But hear me out!' he said, raising a forefinger. 'My delightful wife took the invitation from my hands and persuaded me it would be a good idea to accept the extension of the olive branch. Now I can't say that she managed to talk me round completely. Just a few days ago I remained reluctant to set foot here. But from the first moment my family and I arrived this evening, we have been given the warmest of welcomes and been treated with such courtesy that I have quite changed my mind about the Buckley-Phipps.'

'Oh, how lovely!' said Lady Buckley-Phipps.

'So I would like to express my gratitude to Lord and Lady Buckley-Phipps for putting an end to the dreadful feud which has divided our families for generations. And I invite you all to join me in a toast. Pick up your glasses, everyone.' He raised his glass above his head and everyone else got to their feet. 'A toast to our wonderful hosts this evening, their family and this wonderful establishment, Fortescue Manor. May our newly repaired bond last for generations to come!'

'Hear, hear!' said Lord Buckley-Phipps and everyone took a sip of their drinks.

Everyone sat down, then Lord Buckley-Phipps stood up again.

'Thank you, Lord Abercromby—'

'You must call me Timothy!'

'Oh, very well. And you may call me Ivan. I would like to thank you, Timothy, for gracing us with your presence. And I would particularly like to thank your dear wife who clearly persuaded you to accept our invitation! When Lucinda first suggested to me that we make friends with our neighbours, I was dead against the idea, just as you were, Timothy. But now we've had such a wonderful evening, I am delighted to consider you a dear friend. You and your family will always be welcome under our roof here at Fortescue Manor.'

This was followed by a round of applause.

'But what about the thirty acres?' said Percy. 'When can we get that back again?'

'Now, Percy, that's forgotten about,' said his father. 'I used to feel extremely embittered about the entire affair, but your mother's talked me round. Thirty acres really isn't worth piffling about. We must let bygones be bygones.'

Chapter Ten

AFTER DINNER, everyone left the dining room and strolled into the saloon. It was a large comfortable room in the centre of the house from which doors led to neighbouring rooms and the entrance hall. The ladies made their way to the drawing room, while the gentlemen headed for the smoking room. Barty took Lottie's arm and led her to the library.

'I need a quick word before I have to show those old books to telltale Percy,' he whispered.

The library was furnished with mahogany bookshelves, a thick carpet and plush seating. Tall windows overlooked the lawn at the front of the house.

'Oh dear, Lottie, help me.' Barty slumped into a chair and loosened his bow tie.

'What's the matter?'

'I'm in love, Lottie! Seriously, deeply and irretrievably in love!'

'With who?'

'Evelyn Abercromby, of course! I have never seen a woman so beautiful, so enchanting, so completely and utterly perfect and delightful.'

'Didn't you say she was a snivelling little girl?'

'That's when I last saw her. When I was about eight years old. But now! She's become a different person!'

'She's grown into an adult.'

'Exactly! And what a beautiful adult she is! I know I shall never stop thinking about her for as long as I live. Oh Lottie, what am I to do?'

Rosie nudged her nose against his leg and he patted her head.

'You could try speaking to her,' said Lottie.

'I can't! I can't find any words. And you know that's completely unlike me.'

'It's very unlike you.'

'What can one say to someone as perfect as Evelyn?'

'Maybe ask her what books she likes reading.'

'And she'll reply with the names of lots of books I've never heard of before. And I wouldn't know what to say about them and I would look so foolish and stupid!'

'You could tell her about the books you've read.'

'I've only read one. The first volume of *Tom Brown's Schooldays*. I'm quite sure Evelyn won't have read that. The only other topic I can think of is the weather, but if I mention that, then Evelyn will think I'm completely dull. People only talk about the weather when they don't know what else to talk about.'

'She likes horses. Maybe you could talk to her about them?'

'I'm worried if I mention horses, then she'll offer to help me improve my riding again. I'll get so embarrassed about that, I really wouldn't know what to say!'

'Why don't you take her up on the offer?'

'But I would be so nervous, I'd fall off! I just know it. She'll go off me in an instant. Perhaps you could speak to her for me.'

'And say what?'

'Tell her what a decent chap I am.'

'No, I'm not doing that.'

'Oh please!'

'No. You must do it yourself.'

'Tell her I'm a decent chap?'

'Just *show* her you're a decent chap.'

'How?'

'I'm sure you'll think of something.'

'Hello?' Percy Abercromby stepped into the room.

'I'll leave you both to it,' said Lottie. 'Enjoy looking at the old books.'

Barty gave a sigh. 'I'm sure we will.'

Chapter Eleven

'YOUR HUSBAND GAVE A LOVELY SPEECH, Lady Abercromby,' said Lady Buckley-Phipps, when Lottie and Rosie arrived in the drawing room.

'You must call me Elizabeth.'

'And you must call me Lucinda. How nice it is to have healed old wounds.'

'It's wonderful. I only wish we had thought of it sooner.'

'Me too! All those wasted years.'

'I think it's marvellous what you two ladies have achieved,' said Mrs Moore. 'And it sounds like you both had to talk your husbands round.'

'We did,' said Lady Abercromby. 'Luckily, Timothy usually does what I say.'

'And the same with Ivan!' chuckled Lady Buckley-Phipps.

Mildred served everyone with glasses of port. She gave Lottie a coy smile as if she thought it was amusing her friend was socialising with important people.

'No port for me, dear,' said the dowager. 'I'm going to retrieve my poor dogs from the gunroom and take them out for an evening stroll.'

'Isn't it a bit late?' said Lady Buckley-Phipps.

'Not at all! What's the time? It's only just after nine. And it's still light outside.' The dowager got up and left the room.

'The Dowager Lady Buckley-Phipps is quite formidable, isn't she?' said Lady Abercromby.

'She certainly is,' said Lady Buckley-Phipps.

'Presumably she has her own house in the grounds of the estate?'

'Yes, she does.'

'That's a good arrangement. I know from experience that it's not easy living with your mother-in-law close at hand.'

'She has her own house and yet she chooses to live here with us in the main house.'

'Oh. I didn't realise you got on so well with her.'

Lady Buckley-Phipps gave a polite smile in reply. 'This is a lovely port, isn't it? Did you have port as good as this on your travels, Roberta?'

'No, I don't think we did. But if we had visited Portugal, then there would have been a possibility. Portugal is where port is from, isn't it?'

'I think so,' said Lady Abercromby. 'Some good friends of ours, the Stapleton-Cottons, were there recently.'

'You know the Stapleton-Cottons?' said Lady Buckley-Phipps. 'They're good friends of ours, too!'

When Mrs Moore added she was also familiar with a Stapleton-Cotton, the conversation moved on to mutual acquaintances.

After a while, Lottie grew bored. She watched the clock on the mantelpiece, wondering how long it would be before everyone could retire for the evening. Evelyn looked bored, too. Rosie walked between them, receiving pats on the head. Then she lay down on the hearthrug and settled into a snooze. Lottie wondered how Barty had got on with showing Percy the old books about battles. Then she felt her eyelids growing heavy as the large meal and the glass of port had a soporific effect. It was only half-past nine. To counter the sleepiness, she sat upright in her seat. It would be extremely bad manners to fall asleep now.

'Oh!'

At first, Lottie thought she'd imagined the noise. Where had it come from?

'Goodness me!'

It was a woman's voice, from beyond the drawing room door. The ladies paused their conversation.

'What was that?' said Lady Buckley-Phipps.

The ladies got to their feet.

'Help!'

'Oh gosh!' Lady Buckley-Phipps was the first to the door, and they followed her out into the saloon.

The Dowager Lady Buckley-Phipps lay sprawled on the floor of the saloon. Her walking stick lay next to her and her three dogs were yapping excitedly.

Harry the footman was crouched beside the old lady, trying to help her up.

The gentlemen had dashed out of the smoking room. 'Mother!' cried out Lord Buckley-Phipps. Within seconds, concerned family and staff surrounded the dowager.

'Oh dear!' she said.

'What happened?'

'Someone knocked me over.'

'*Knocked you over*?' cried out Lord Buckley-Phipps. 'Who?'

The dowager was now on her feet and Lady Buckley-Phipps gave her the walking stick.

'I don't know who it was,' she said. 'It was all so fast, I didn't see. They went that way.' She pointed at the entrance hall.

Lottie watched on, unsure of what to do. Then she

noticed Harry the footman tug at Lord Buckley-Phipps' sleeve and point at the library door.

They both went into the room, then reappeared moments later.

Lord Buckley-Phipps' face was ashen. 'I need everyone's attention!' he announced. 'I'm afraid there's been a dreadful accident!'

Chapter Twelve

Percy Abercromby was dead.

Everyone sat in the drawing room in stunned silence as Detective Inspector Lloyd paced in front of the fireplace, puffing on a pipe. He was a short, stocky man with no neck. He had neatly parted hair, a thick moustache, and his brows were locked in a permanent frown.

Lottie felt great sympathy for the Abercromby family. Lady Abercromby's eyes were ringed with red and her husband's expression was fixed with shock. Evelyn sat next to her mother, tightly clasping her hand.

Everyone was present except Barty. Lottie couldn't understand where he'd got to.

'So to summarise the evening's events,' said the detective. 'Young Mr Abercromby has been found deceased in the library. He was attacked with an ornamental dagger which I'm told serves as a letter opener for Lord Buckley-Phipps.'

'I didn't use it very often,' said Lord Buckley-Phipps. 'It's quite a cumbersome item and I use a much smaller one day-to-day. I last saw it in my desk drawer and I have no idea how it got—'

Detective Inspector Lloyd raised his pipe to halt him. 'Thank you, my lord. I shall take detailed statements from everyone in due course. At the present time, I would like to establish the exact chain of events.'

'Of course, Lloyd. Do continue.'

'I think the chain of events is quite obvious!' cried out Lady Abercromby. 'They've murdered my son!' She pointed at the Buckley-Phipps family who were sat on the opposite side of the room to her, her husband and daughter. 'They invited us here so they could murder our heir!'

'Not true!' said Lady Buckley-Phipps. 'No one in this house would ever dream of doing such a thing!'

The detective raised his pipe again. 'Ladies. Please. I understand emotions are running high, but we must do our best to remain calm. I need an accurate record of what exactly happened here this evening. Now, from what I understand, the crime came to everyone's attention when the Dowager Lady Buckley-Phipps was knocked over by the assailant in the saloon.'

'That's right,' said Lord Buckley-Phipps. He turned to the dowager. 'What did you see of the assailant, Mother?'

'Nothing! He knocked into me from the left and over I went. While I was on the floor, I was aware of a figure running to the entrance hall. But I didn't exactly see the person. It was just movement and footsteps. My first thought was that it was one of the servants and I wanted to admonish them for running about the place and being so careless. But the fall knocked all the breath from me. It was only when I recovered a little, that I was able to call out for help.'

'Did the person say anything to you?' asked the detective.

'There was a brief muttered apology. He clearly regretted what he'd done. But he was keen to get away. And now I've learned what he did, I'm not surprised!'

'When did you realise Mr Abercromby had been attacked in the library?'

'When everyone was talking about it. I had no idea Mr Abercromby was in there when the stranger crashed into me.'

'So the person who discovered Mr Abercromby in the library was the footman, Harry Lewis,' said the detective. 'Am I right?'

'Yes, he's the person who discovered him,' said Lord Buckley-Phipps.

'Very good. I shall speak with him next. Now we need to establish the time when this happened. What was the time when the Dowager Lady Buckley-Phipps was found on the floor?'

'I think it was about half-past nine,' said Lady Buckley-Phipps. 'We dined at seven and left the dining room just after nine. The ladies came here into the drawing room and the gentlemen went to the smoking room. The exception was Barty, Percy and Miss Sprigg. Although Miss Sprigg joined us here after a few minutes.'

'And then I took my dogs out for a walk,' said the dowager. 'It's something I do every evening. I was just on my way back to the drawing room when that ragamuffin knocked me over.'

'Percy spoke to Barty Buckley-Phipps in the library,' said Lord Abercromby. 'Lord Buckley-Phipps suggested he showed some books about battles to Percy. That's how the plan was hatched!'

'There was no plan to do something so awful!' said Lord Buckley-Phipps. 'It was merely a—'

'Sorry to interrupt, my lord,' said Detective Inspector Lloyd. 'But where is Mr Buckley-Phipps now?'

Everyone glanced around as if seeking the answer from someone else.

'We don't know,' said Lady Buckley-Phipps.

'Has he been seen since the murder?'

'No.'

'Interesting.'

Lottie felt her stomach turn cold. Could Barty really have murdered Percy? She couldn't imagine him doing such a thing.

'Let's return to the person who knocked over the Dowager Lady Buckley-Phipps,' said Detective Inspector Lloyd. 'He ran out through the main entrance?'

'That's where I saw him go,' said the dowager.

'Did anyone chase after him?'

'All the men did,' said Lord Buckley-Phipps. 'Gentlemen and servants alike. But there was no sign of the man.'

'No sign of the man and no sign of Barty Buckley-Phipps, either,' said the detective. 'Rather suspicious, wouldn't you say?'

Chapter Thirteen

THE DRAWING ROOM door opened and Barty Buckley-Phipps strolled in.

'Hullo?' he said. 'What's going on? I saw the police car parked outside the house. Has there been a robbery?'

'No Barty, it's terrible!' said his mother, stepping over to embrace him. 'Poor Percy has been murdered!'

'Percy?' Barty's face paled. 'When?'

'When he was in the library with you,' snarled Lord Abercromby.

'With me? He was perfectly alive when he was with me.'

'Was he alive when you left the library?' asked Detective Inspector Lloyd.

'Of course! I'd never seen him more alive.' He staggered over to a chair and sat down. 'I can't believe he's dead. When did this happen?'

'About half an hour ago,' said Lady Buckley-Phipps. 'Someone attacked Percy in the library, then knocked over your grandmother as he made his escape.'

'He *knocked Granny over*?' Barty seemed more horrified by this than he did by the murder. 'Are you alright, Granny?'

'Not too bad, thank you, Barty. A little bruised.'

'It must have been the man I saw earlier!' he said.

'What man?' asked Lord Buckley-Phipps.

'The man loitering beneath the oak tree near the deer park.'

'But we searched everywhere for the man who did this and saw no one! What did he look like?'

'I only saw him from a distance. He wore dark clothing, and he was a bit scruffy looking. Not a gentleman, I assumed he was a labourer.'

'And you didn't challenge him?' said Lord Buckley-Phipps.

'No. He was too far away, and I just thought he was someone who'd been doing some work on the estate.'

'When did you see him?'

'Just after I left the library.'

'What time did you leave the library?' asked the detective.

'I don't know.'

'You don't know?'

'It was before everything happened, that's for sure.'

'Can you tell us what happened while you were in the library with Percy Abercromby?'

'Very well.' Barty cleared his throat. 'I went there after dinner, just as Father had instructed, because I had to show Percy some old war books. He turned up a few minutes later.'

'What time was this?'

'Just after nine. Five past, maybe. Anyway, I showed him the old books and then I left and went outside.'

'Why didn't you join the rest of us in the smoking room?' asked Lord Abercromby.

Detective Inspector Lloyd raised an eyebrow and turned to Barty. 'You were supposed to go to the smoking room?'

'I don't know if I was supposed to. But it was where the gentlemen had gathered after dinner.'

'But you didn't join them?'

'No. I decided to go for a walk.'

'Why?'

There was a pause. 'I needed to clear my head,' said Barty eventually.

'After you showed Percy Abercromby the books?'

'Yes.'

'Why?'

Barty cleared his throat again. 'There's no easy way of putting this. But we had a bit of a row.'

Lady Abercromby gasped. 'I knew it! You murdered him!'

'Please allow me to find out more, Lady Abercromby,' said the detective. He turned back to Barty. 'What was the row about?'

'It was nothing, just a petty argument, which is quite meaningless now that Percy's no longer with us.'

'It's important that I understand what the argument was about, Mr Buckley-Phipps.'

'I really would prefer not to say.'

'But it's extremely important you tell me.'

'Would I be able to tell you privately?' He glanced around the room, biting his lip. Lord and Lady Abercromby glared at him.

'Very well,' said the detective. 'We can discuss this during the detailed interviews.'

'He's hiding something!' said Lord Abercromby. 'He's guilty!'

The detective raised his pipe. 'I must ask you to remain calm, my lord. I shall get to the bottom of this.'

'You'd better do!'

'Mr Buckley-Phipps,' said the detective. 'I urge you to think about how long you were in the library for.'

'About ten minutes.'

'So you think you left at quarter-past nine?'

'Yes, probably. And then I went for a long walk around the deer park and the lake.'

Detective Inspector Lloyd turned to everyone else in the room. 'Did anyone here see Percy Abercromby alive after quarter-past nine?'

People shook their heads, and no one responded.

'I see,' said the detective. 'It seems that you, Mr Buckley-Phipps, were the last person to see that young man alive.'

Chapter Fourteen

LOTTIE TOOK Rosie for a short walk in the gardens while she waited to be interviewed by Detective Inspector Lloyd. It was dark now, but there was some light from the crescent moon high in the sky. Rosie sniffed at a flower bed filled with lavender and Lottie breathed in the calming scent.

She couldn't believe Barty would have harmed Percy Abercromby. But who else would have had the opportunity? She thought of Harry the footman. He'd been close by because he'd helped the dowager after she'd been knocked over. Perhaps he was the one who'd committed the crime?

But the dowager had reported that the man who'd knocked her over had run out of the main entrance. Was he the same man who Barty had claimed to have seen beneath the tree?

There was a lot to think about.

A shout disturbed her thoughts. It came from the servants' courtyard near the kitchen steps. The voice belonged to a man and sounded as though it had been raised in anger. Then she heard something move over the gravel. In the dim light, she caught sight of someone on a bicycle. They were moving quickly, as if keen to get away. The bicycle squeaked as it moved. In no time, they rounded the corner of the house and were gone. Presumably heading in the direction of the long driveway.

Detective Inspector Lloyd had instructed everyone to remain at the house for the time being. So who was leaving on a bicycle? And why were they leaving at this late hour?

Lottie met Mrs Moore in the saloon when she returned to the house.

'It's all rather unfortunate, isn't it, Lottie?' Mrs Moore spoke in a hushed, reverent tone. 'This evening was the first time in almost three hundred years that the Buckley-Phipps and Abercromby families have met on good terms. And then one of the Abercrombys is murdered under this very roof! Just dreadful. Lucinda is in despair. But not as much despair as poor Lord and Lady Abercromby! I can understand why they're pointing the finger at Barty, it makes sense, doesn't it? He argued with their son in the library and he was the last person to see him alive. I can't imagine the young man doing such a thing, though.'

'And if Barty was the murderer, then I don't think he would have admitted to having argued with Percy,' said Lottie.

'Now that's a good point. Why would he admit to discord between them if he was trying to cover up a crime?'

A young constable approached. 'Detective Inspector Lloyd will see you now, Mrs Moore and Miss Sprigg. He's conducting his interviews in the music room.'

The stocky detective invited Lottie and Mrs Moore to join him at a round table with red and gold upholstered chairs. A piano sat on one side and a harp on the other. A clock ticked noisily on the mantelpiece.

'You have a dog with you,' he said, puffing on his pipe. 'A corgi. My mother always had corgis.'

'How nice,' said Mrs Moore.

'They never liked me very much,' he said, patting Rosie on the head. 'But this one does.'

'Then you're extremely privileged, Detective.'

'Am I? Well, that's flattering indeed. It's an honour to be liked by an animal, don't you think? They don't like everybody.'

'They certainly don't.'

The detective opened his notebook. 'Let's get on with things. I've got a lot of people to speak to. And I need to somehow determine which one of them plunged a dagger into Percy Abercromby's back.'

'His back?' said Mrs Moore.

'I'm afraid so. Cowardly, isn't it? Now can you tell me when you last saw the victim alive?'

'At dinner in the dining room,' said Mrs Moore. 'And I understood he was going to look at some books about war in the library afterwards.'

'I saw him in the library,' said Lottie.

'Did you?' The detective raised an interested eyebrow. 'When was this?'

Lottie explained she'd had a conversation with Barty in the library. 'And our conversation ended when Mr Abercromby entered the room,' she added.

'And what did he say?'

'From memory he said "hello" and I told them I would leave them to it. I then left the room.'

'Did you hear the argument between them?'

'No.'

'And how was Mr Abercromby when you saw him?'

'I didn't know him very well, but he seemed his normal self. Just as he'd been at dinner.'

'And Mr Buckley-Phipps?'

'He was his normal self, too.' She felt the need to be honest about his mood and added, 'I think he may have been slightly reluctant to show Mr Abercromby the books.'

'Reluctant you say? Interesting.' He wrote something down, and Lottie hoped she wasn't getting Barty into even more trouble. 'Why was he reluctant?'

'He and Percy didn't get on very well at school. Only because they were quite different personalities.'

'Very interesting indeed.' The detective wrote some more in his notebook, and Lottie felt a sinking sensation in her stomach. Why was she being so honest? Her words were surely making Barty seem even more guilty. 'I know he wouldn't have harmed Percy,' she said. 'I've known Barty for five years. I used to work here as a maid. He's known for getting into scrapes, but there's no malice about him whatsoever.'

The detective nodded and sat back in his chair. 'This is all very interesting indeed. When did you next see Mr Buckley-Phipps?'

'After you arrived this evening. When he arrived in the drawing room after returning from his walk.'

'And after you left the library, Miss Sprigg, where did you go then?'

'To the drawing room where the ladies had gone after dinner.'

'And Mrs Moore,' said the detective. 'Where did you go after dinner?'

'Directly to the drawing room. And there we stayed until we heard the Dowager Lady Buckley-Phipps crying out for help.'

'So you saw no one entering or leaving the library?'

'No, because we were in the drawing room.'

'Did you see anyone entering or leaving the study?'

'No. We couldn't have done because we—'

'Were in the drawing room. Of course.'

'We really didn't see anything, Detective,' said Mrs Moore.

'Are you aware of anyone who wished to harm Percy Abercromby?'

'No. But I hardly knew the young gentleman. I don't live in this area, I live in London. And before that I was in America. This is my sister's home and I've merely been a visitor over the years.'

'I remember occasionally seeing Percy Abercromby in Lowton Chorley when he was younger,' said Lottie. 'But because of the feud between the Buckley-Phipps and Abercromby families, no one in this household had much to do with him. As far as I'm aware.'

'As far as you are *aware*, Miss Sprigg. That's an interesting point,' said the detective. 'Because I feel sure the murderer knows this house well. How else would they have known where to find a deadly ornamental letter opener? And although there's been a feud between the two families for centuries, someone in this house felt aggrieved enough by Percy Abercromby to murder him. Why? Did he say something wrong at dinner?'

'I don't recall that he did,' said Mrs Moore. 'And even if he had, it wouldn't warrant murdering him.'

'Exactly. So someone here had something to do with him. And I'm afraid you all must be under suspicion. Including the servants.'

'I don't think we all need to be under suspicion, Detective,' said Mrs Moore. 'The ladies who were in the drawing room can all provide alibis for each other. As can the gentlemen who were in the smoking room together. I'm sure I could say the same for the servants. Establishing alibis for all those people will rule them out quickly. That will then surely only leave you with a handful of suspects?'

The detective gave a sniff. 'I suppose it would. But I begin by suspecting everyone, Mrs Moore. And then I go through a careful process of elimination.'

'Perhaps you could ask Miss Sprigg to help you, Detective?'

'Help?' His brow knotted into a deep frown. 'Thank you for the offer, Mrs Moore, but I think I shall manage quite well as it is.'

'You don't realise what this young lady is capable of. On our recent travels to Europe and north Africa, she helped catch no fewer than five murderers.'

'*Five?*'

'That's right.'

'I had no idea it was so dangerous abroad.'

'It's not. We just happened to be in the wrong places at the wrong times. Actually, it was a good thing we were there because Lottie solved the cases.'

'With some help, I expect.'

'Only a little help.'

'Well, that is impressive indeed.'

'It is. You wouldn't think it to look at her, would you? Such a quiet, unassuming type. But she has a remarkable brain and a thorough eye for detail. And she doesn't forget a thing! It has to be seen to be believed.'

Lottie felt her cheeks burn red and willed Mrs Moore to stop talking about her.

'Well, I'm impressed,' said the detective. 'It sounds like you did some excellent work while you were abroad, Miss Sprigg. From what I hear, the investigative abilities of detectives on the continent are rather roughshod. They probably need all the help they can get. Don't forget you're back in Britain now, where we take great pride in our law and order.

The first modern police force in the world was founded here! I think it's quite clear that we know what we're doing. Not only do I have many experienced police officers to call on, but I can also ask Scotland Yard for assistance if I need it.'

He paused to puff out a plume of pipe smoke, then turned to Lottie. 'So there's no need to concern yourself with this crime, Miss Sprigg. You can spend your time on needlework or sketching instead. This place has some pretty views, doesn't it? If I were a young lady, I know I'd derive great pleasure from strolling around the grounds with my sketchbook and capturing attractive scenes with my pencil and paper. So much better than the sordid business of crime. In fact, I'm quite opposed to ladies occupying themselves with such things, it's not good for their minds. They're simply not built for it.'

HARRY STIFLED a yawn as he sat in the music room with Detective Inspector Lloyd. The clock on the mantelpiece showed it was past one o'clock in the morning. The detective had interviewed all the important people first and had left the servants until the end.

'What's your full name, young man?' asked the detective.

'Harry Lewis.'

'And you're a footman.'

'Yes.'

The detective eyed him for a moment. Was he expecting him to call him sir? Harry had to do enough bowing and scraping in his job, he didn't see why he should do the same with a policeman. Even if he was a detective inspector.

'How old are you?'

'Twenty-three.'

'How long have you worked here?'

'Nearly a year.'

'And do you enjoy your job?'

'It's alright.'

'Just alright? The Buckley-Phipps family is extremely distinguished.'

Harry shrugged his shoulders. He considered the Buckley-Phipps family to be like any other. They'd merely had the luck to be born into vast wealth.

The Abercromby family were just the same. And the sight of Percy Abercromby that evening had enraged him. A few months had passed since he'd last seen him, but the anger hadn't passed. He could feel the sensations of hurt and betrayal again. Pain in his chest and a weakness in his knees. Percy Abercromby had known what he'd done but he hadn't cared.

'What were you doing just before the Dowager Lady Buckley-Phipps was knocked over?'

'I was making sure everything had been tidied away in the dining room after dinner.'

'You weren't in the library?'

'No!'

'Because you found Percy Abercromby in the library.'

'Only after I'd helped the dowager to her feet.'

'You were perfectly placed to commit the murder. You could have attacked Mr Abercromby then claimed to have found him.'

'That didn't happen!'

The detective puffed on his pipe. 'Was anyone with you in the dining room?'

'Not at that time.'

'Doesn't the butler make sure everything has been tidied away?'

'Yes. I was making sure everything was in order before Mr Duxbury came in to check.'

'The Dowager Lady Buckley-Phipps was knocked over at half-past nine. I've spoken to Mr Duxbury, and he was downstairs at the time. He'd already checked the dining room by half-past nine.'

Harry felt his stomach give a turn. He hadn't realised the detective would be quite so thorough. 'Perhaps I'm mistaken about the time.'

'Were you in the dining room when the dowager was knocked to the ground?'

'I suppose I must have been.'

'You *suppose*? You were first on the scene to help her, so you must have been close by. The dining room is next to the saloon where she fell. The other servants took longer to arrive because they had to run up the stairs.'

'Yes, I was in the dining room.'

'So no *suppose* about it?'

'No.'

'And what were you doing in there?'

'Making sure everything was tidy.'

'Even though Mr Duxbury had already made sure of that?'

'I couldn't have realised he'd already done it.'

'But surely everything looked immaculate in there if the butler had already checked the room?'

'Yes, it was. But I didn't realise until I went in there.'

Harry's palms felt clammy, but he did his best to remain calm.

'Did you know Percy Abercromby?'

'No.' It was half the truth.

'You didn't know him at all?'

'I think I saw him in the village a few times.' The tightness in his chest returned. And the anger. Then an image flashed into his mind. Percy laughing as he strolled along the high street. Harry's hands balled into fists beneath the table.

'So you checked a room which had already been checked?'

'Yes it seems so.'

'How odd.'

It was clear the detective suspected he'd been up to no good. He couldn't adequately account for where he was at the time of Percy Abercromby's murder. He'd thought an excuse about checking the dining room would have been enough, but the detective had already checked the details with Mr Duxbury. There was no obvious reason Harry would have been in the dining room at half-past nine. And because there had been no one else in the dining room at that time, the detective no doubt suspected he'd been in the library.

There was someone he could ask to provide an alibi for him, but it was too risky. It was possible he'd end up in even more trouble than he already was.

Something had happened which he felt pleased about, though.

Percy Abercromby was dead.

'OH LOTTIE, I can't sleep! It's so awful!' Mildred perched on the end of Lottie's bed next to Rosie. 'That poor Percy Abercromby! He didn't deserve something like that.'

'No, he didn't,' said Lottie. She sat up in bed with a shawl over her shoulders. 'I'm struggling to understand who could have done it.'

'Me too. It should be easy to work out, shouldn't it? There weren't many people about when it happened. Obviously there was Mr Buckley-Phipps.'

'I don't think it could have been him.'

'Me neither. And then there was Harry, the footman. He found Mr Abercromby in the library.'

'Do you think he could have done it?'

'I don't know.'

'Me neither. I don't know him very well, but he's been unfriendly towards me since my return.'

'He's probably jealous.'

'Of what?'

'You're not a maid anymore, and he still has to wait on people. I don't think he's suited for his job, he's always

70

moaning about it. I don't understand why he doesn't go and work in the biscuit factory instead.'

'Hopefully he will. Where was he when Percy Abercromby was attacked?'

'He's told everyone he was in the dining room, but I don't know what he was doing in there because we'd finished in the dining room by then.'

'So what was he up to?'

'I don't know. I don't like Harry very much, but I don't think he could be a murderer.'

'Maybe not. And just because he's unfriendly, that doesn't mean he's capable of carrying out murder.'

'Who else is there? The dowager. But she couldn't have done it. She's an old lady.'

'And the murderer knocked her over when he left.'

'Of course, the murderer left. So it can't have been Harry, can it? He was there to help the dowager.'

'Unless he ran off, then returned to help her.'

Mildred shook her head. 'No, I can't imagine that.'

Lottie told Mildred about the person on the bicycle she'd seen leaving the servants' courtyard. 'Do you know who it could have been?'

'No. Edward the footman has a bicycle, but I don't know why he would go off on it late at night. Especially when the detective told us we all had to stay in the house and be interviewed. The only other people who ride bicycles are the delivery boys, but they're only about in the day, aren't they? None of them have got any reason to be visiting the house at night.'

'Whoever it was must have spoken to someone from the house,' said Lottie. 'Presumably someone who was in the servants' courtyard.'

'Well that's mysterious,' said Mildred. 'I can ask about, but I don't know who that could have been.'

Chapter Seventeen

BREAKFAST THE FOLLOWING morning was subdued. The usual array of dishes was presented on the sideboard, but Lottie had little appetite.

'How are my sister and her husband this morning?' Mrs Moore asked Mr Duxbury the butler as she spooned kedgeree onto her plate.

'His lordship breakfasted early and is currently meeting with Detective Inspector Lloyd. I haven't yet heard how her ladyship is faring this morning.'

'I hope she's alright. I'll knock on her door a little later.' She took a seat opposite Lottie. 'I can't even begin to consider how poor Lord and Lady Abercromby are this morning. And their dear daughter, Evelyn. Such a tragedy.'

'It is.' Lottie picked up her knife and fork and attempted to tackle the small portion of scrambled egg and toast in front of her.

'A letter has arrived for you this morning, Mrs Moore.' The butler handed her an envelope.

'Thank you. I wonder who this can be from? Few people know I'm staying here.'

She tore open the envelope, and Lottie watched her face fall as she read the letter.

'Oh dear,' she said.

'What is it?'

'It's from Mr Sykes.'

Lottie had never heard the name before. 'Who's he?'

'A man who once wished to become my fourth husband.'

'I don't recognise his name.'

'That's because I choose to mention him as little as possible. The man is a nuisance.'

'Does he live locally?'

'No, but his sister does. I met him at a gathering in London last year and we discovered our sisters lived within a few miles of each other in Shropshire. He seemed to think the coincidence meant we should marry. But I know he was only interested in me because I'm rich.'

'Surely that's not true?'

'I'm not being self-deprecating, Lottie. I know I can be a perfectly delightful and charming person. But I learned long ago how to spot the people who are after one's money. As I understand it, Sykes inherited some money, and he tries to live off it. But I think the money's been running low for a few years. He needs a rich wife and I've turned him down once already.'

'But he's still persisting?'

'It seems so. I thought I'd seen the back of him, but sadly not.'

'How annoying! Do you mind me asking what his letter says?'

'Not at all. You can read it if you like, Lottie.'

Mrs Moore passed it across the table to her.

My dear Roberta

. . .

I was most delighted to hear from my dear sister, Joanne, that you have returned from your travels abroad. She mentioned the fact to me as we were recalling the delightful party at Mr Jonathan Blooming's home in Belgravia. I trust your memories of that evening remain as agreeable as mine!

I would consider it most unfortunate if our paths failed to cross while we're both staying in glorious Shropshire. I sincerely hope circumstances will allow us to meet. Joanne assures me you are most welcome to visit us at her home at a time of your choosing.

I hope such an arrangement would be pleasing to you and I look forward to your reply.

Mr Bertrand Sykes

'Are you going to reply with an excuse?' Lottie asked, passing the letter back to her employer.

'No.' Mrs Moore screwed the letter up into a ball, picked up her lorgnette and surveyed the room. 'Where's the nearest wastepaper basket?'

'You're not going to reply at all?'

'No. There's no need. And besides, he'll presumably hear of the tragedy here soon enough and realise he has to leave me alone. Ah, there we are!'

Mrs Moore hurled the balled-up letter across the room. It bounced off the wainscoting and landed in the wastepaper basket.

Lottie clapped. 'Great shot!'

Barty entered the breakfast room, looking glum and pale.

'How are you Barty?' said Mrs Moore.

'Awful. Everyone thinks I'm a murderer.'

'Nonsense! No one thinks that.'

'They do! All because I had an argument with Percy.'

'What did you argue with him about?' Lottie asked.

'He confronted me about his sister, Evelyn. He told me to stop staring at her with my great googly eyes.'

'Googly?'

'Yes. He hadn't grown up at all. He was still using words from our schooldays. I told him I wasn't staring at his sister and that I don't have googly eyes. And do you know what he said after that? He said he was going to tell his father about me staring. He was a telltale until the bitter end! Oh dear, I feel awful talking about him in this way because the poor chap has been murdered.'

'Well it's quite clear the pair of you didn't get along,' said Mrs Moore. 'But that doesn't mean you meant him any harm.'

'Try telling Detective Inspector Lloyd that. He suspects me and I've not got a pleasant history with him.'

'Oh dear, what happened?'

'We were just playing a bit of sport.'

'What sort of sport?'

'Well, I don't know if you remember this, Auntie. But years ago, when Detective Inspector Lloyd was a constable, he used to go about Lowton Chorley on his bicycle, thinking very highly of himself. Some friends and I decided on a competition to see who could knock his helmet off with an apple.'

'That's not a very sensible competition, Barty.'

'I realise that now, Auntie. But I was only nine or ten at the time. And, unfortunately for me, I was an excellent shot.'

'You succeeded in knocking off his helmet?'

'Yes, from a distance of thirty yards. The helmet came clean off and bounced across the road. Lloyd couldn't have done his chinstrap up very tightly. The next thing I knew, I was hauled off to the police station by the lobe of my ear and Father was summoned.'

'I can't imagine your father was very happy.'

'No, he wasn't. Although he was impressed with how well I'd hit the target. He wrote a letter to my games master ordering him to put me in the first eleven school cricket team. I ended up setting a new school record for taking the most wickets. And I think the record still stands to this day. None of that helps me now though, does it? Detective Inspector Lloyd doesn't like me. I'm doomed!'

Chapter Eighteen

MORNING SUNLIGHT STREAMED in through the windows of the music room. Barty sat rigidly in his chair and eyed Detective Inspector Lloyd cautiously.

'Thank you for seeing me again, Mr Buckley-Phipps,' said the detective. 'We had a chat yesterday evening, but I'd like to go over it again this morning, if I may.'

'Go over it again?'

'Yes, just to check the consistency of your story.'

'Story? It's the truth!'

'If it's the truth, then it will be consistent. If it's a tale which you've invented, then I'll be able to catch you out.'

'I see.' Barty felt his heart thudding in his chest. He felt sure the detective would be able to catch him out quite easily.

'The person who carried out the attack on Mr Abercromby was familiar with the layout of this house,' said the detective. 'The killer knew that a sharp ornamental letter opener was in the desk drawer in your father's study. Few people could have known that, could they?'

'I suppose not.'

'Did you know it was there?'

'I knew my father owned a rather lethal-looking letter opener because I liked to play with it as a child. It looked like a proper sword and I used it in my pirate games. But when Nanny saw me with it, it was taken off me. I don't understand why he owned a letter opener which was that large and sharp. A much smaller one would have done. In fact, I think he owns a smaller one. The ornamental one was a gift.'

'So you knew about the letter opener.'

'Yes. But I didn't murder Percy!'

'Tell me again what happened in the library.'

'I showed him where the boring old war books were, then I prepared to leave the room. But he began accusing me of making eyes at his sister.'

'Were you?'

'I was merely struck by how much she had changed since I last saw her.'

'When did you last see her?'

'When I was eight.'

'Some time ago.'

'Exactly.'

'Do continue.'

'I know I glanced at his sister a few times, surprised by the change.' Barty didn't want to admit how completely entranced he'd been by her. It seemed weak to admit to the detective that he'd fallen in love.

'So Mr Abercromby mistook the glances you made at his sister as making eyes at her.'

'Exactly!'

'Then what happened?'

'I defended myself the best I could. But not by murdering him, I should add.'

'Did you come to blows?'

'No! I've never come to blows with another chap in my entire life.'

'Did he attack you?'

'No! We merely exchanged angry words, but it went on and on and I had to give up on it and walk away. His mind wouldn't be changed on the matter. I suppose he felt protective of his sister so I can understand his annoyance. But have you realised something, Detective? If I'd planned to murder Percy, then I would have needed to fetch the letter opener from the study before I met him in the library. How would I have managed that?'

'You tell me.'

'I couldn't have managed it! There wasn't time. And how could I have known he was going to accuse me of something? I had no idea an argument was about to begin.'

'Perhaps you prepared yourself with the weapon just in case.'

'No, I didn't, Detective. Percy took me by surprise launching into an attack on me like that. I wasn't prepared for an argument at all. I'd merely been expecting a quick, dull conversation about some old war books. Then I planned to join the other men in the smoking room.'

'But you went outside.'

'Yes. I needed to get out into the gardens to cool my head.'

'Did you bump into your grandmother when you left the library?'

'No. There was no one else around. And besides, why would I bump into my own grandmother? I would have ensured I avoided her.'

'Perhaps you were in a hurry?'

'I was in no hurry at all.'

'Are you sure? You said you were angry when you left the library and needed to clear your head.'

'Yes, but I wasn't in a desperate hurry. Not like the murderer must have been. Presumably he wanted to get away as quickly as possible.'

'Did you see anyone go into the library after you left?'

'No.'

'And which route did you take to get outside?'

'I went into the saloon and then went out by the entrance hall.'

'Which is the route the attacker also took.'

'It's the most obvious route, I suppose.'

'Were you the man who the Dowager Lady Buckley-Phipps saw leaving the house?'

'No, I can't have been. She wasn't there at the time. And I certainly wouldn't have knocked over my own grandmother!'

'What time did you leave the library?'

'About twenty-past nine, I think. I believe that's ten minutes before the attacker knocked my grandmother over. So it can't have been me, I'd already left the house by then.'

'So you left the library at twenty-past nine and you went out into the gardens at the front of the house.'

'Yes.'

'I'm told your grandmother was out walking her dogs at that time. Did you see her?'

'No. But that's not a surprise because she was probably in the kitchen garden. She likes to walk her dogs there and, if they're lucky, they catch a rabbit. I didn't go near the kitchen garden, I turned left and went out across the deer park.'

'Are you sure you left the house by the main entrance?'

'Yes.'

'Because the library has a set of doors which opens directly onto the gardens at the front.'

'Yes, it does.'

'And we found one of the doors was slightly ajar.'

'Well, I can account for that.'

'How?'

'Percy must have been peering out of the library windows because he saw me leave by the main entrance. He opened the door and called me a wimp for walking away from him. I have to admit that it took all my strength not to march back over to him and knock his teeth out.'

'So he didn't close the door properly after he hurled the insult?'

'No, and that's not terribly surprising. The library doors can be a little stiff and it's not always easy to close them properly. You tend to think you've closed them and then realise you haven't done so at all.'

'So you didn't leave the library by those doors?'

'No.'

'Why not?'

'Because I know the doors are stiff and temperamental. Instinctively I went via the main entrance.'

The detective sat back in his chair and narrowed his eyes. Barty didn't like the way he was looking him up and down.

'You and Percy Abercromby were at school together, weren't you?'

'Yes.'

'Were you friends at school?'

'No. We had little in common. He was studious, and I wasn't.'

'Did the family feud cause a problem between you and Percy at school?'

'No, I don't think either of us gave it any thought. It was something our parents talked about, but we weren't bothered. He had his friends, and I had mine. Then he went to Cambridge, and I went to Oxford. When he turned up here yesterday evening, it was the first time I'd seen him in a year or two.'

'You were kicked out of Oxford, weren't you?'

'It was a misunderstanding which I plan to sort out with them in September.'

The detective puffed out a plume of pipe smoke. 'I've

known you for a number of years, Mr Buckley-Phipps, and you were always the sort of boy to get into trouble.'

'I apologise for the apple-throwing incident. I was young and foolish.'

'But it wasn't just the apple-throwing incident, was it? Throughout your youth you were known for japes and tomfoolery.'

'And most of it harmless fun, Detective! I realise I've blotted my copybook on many occasions, but I'm not a murderer! That's quite a different sort of chap altogether. I can't pretend Percy Abercromby and I were friends, because we weren't. We had a terrible row yesterday evening, and I felt tempted to hit him. But I didn't, because I'm not that sort of fellow. I could never have attacked him in that brutal manner with a dagger! I find that sort of thing unfathomable and unthinkable.'

Chapter Nineteen

'Oh, Barty's been with the detective for ages now!' lamented Lady Buckley-Phipps. 'He's going to be arrested, isn't he?'

'I don't see why he should be, Lucinda,' said Mrs Moore. 'I'm sure he's innocent of any wrongdoing.'

They sat in the morning room and Mildred was serving them coffee. Lottie thought she looked tired after being awake most of the night worrying about the murder.

'But the detective suspects Barty,' said Lady Buckley-Phipps. 'I know it!' She looked as tired as Mildred and the dark circles beneath her eyes complemented the sombre grey dress she was wearing.

'It's because he had a disagreement with Percy,' said Mrs Moore. 'And he doesn't have an alibi for the time of Percy's murder. But—'

'But that's all the police need, isn't it? That's enough to convince them he's the murderer!'

Lottie knew the circumstances didn't look good for Barty. He would have known about the ornamental letter opener in his father's study, and he would have been angered by Percy

Abercromby's confrontation. The pair had disliked each other since their schooldays.

Was Barty capable of murder? It was difficult to believe he would do such a thing. Could he have crashed into his grand-mother and left her sprawled on the floor? Lottie found this difficult to believe, too. But perhaps he'd been so consumed by rage that he'd lost his mind for a moment. Was that possible?

'My boy would never have done such a thing,' said Lord Buckley-Phipps. 'And don't misunderstand me, I've been the first to criticise the young man and the scrapes he's got himself into over the years. But commit murder? He isn't capable of it. He's been brave to admit that he argued with Percy shortly before his death. And I can imagine how angry Barty must have been. That Percy was an infuriating young man! I'd have gladly punched his lights out myself. Ten times over! I wouldn't have murdered him though, I shall make that clear now. But neither would Barty. I can understand the police have a job to do, but if they detain him for much longer, then they'll have me to answer to. It's patently obvious Barty isn't guilty.'

'We need some witnesses,' said Mrs Moore. 'Surely someone must have seen him go in or out of the library. And he must have been seen walking around the grounds. It's time to put an appeal out to all the staff. Someone will have seen something.'

'If only Barty hadn't stormed off outside and just returned to the smoking room,' said Lord Buckley-Phipps. 'All the gentlemen could have vouched for him then. Including Lord Abercromby! And now he's one of the people who's convinced Barty murdered his son.'

'And what are the police doing about the man Barty saw under the oak tree?' said Lady Buckley-Phipps. 'Why aren't they out there looking for him? It's easy to blame Barty for everything because, well... he's the sort of boy we've always blamed for everything.'

'He hasn't helped himself over the years,' said her husband. 'In fact, I'd go far enough to say he's his own worst enemy. But he's entirely innocent and I shall take this up with the chief constable if need be.'

'Oh, what a mess!' wailed Lady Buckley-Phipps. 'Our attempt to mend the feud was a disaster! In fact, it's made everything worse! The Abercrombys have lost their only heir and they're blaming us!'

'Significantly worse than a disagreement over thirty acres of land, isn't it?' said Lord Buckley-Phipps. 'What an absolute disaster. I should never have let you talk me into it, Lucinda.'

'You're saying it's my fault?'

'No, not completely your fault. But if the Abercrombys hadn't been here, then Percy wouldn't have been murdered.'

'But it had nothing to do with me inviting them here for dinner!' said Lady Buckley-Phipps, pulling a handkerchief from her sleeve. 'I only ever tried to do my best!' She dissolved into tears and Mrs Moore moved to her side and took her hand.

'Now, now, Lucinda. You can't possibly blame yourself. Perhaps Percy would have been murdered regardless?' said Mrs Moore. 'Maybe not under your roof, but perhaps someone had been after him for a while? Then they finally found their opportunity here at Fortescue Manor. What do you think, Lottie?'

'It's a possibility, I suppose. We'd need to find out who bore a grudge against him.'

'Yes, we would. And you're very good at finding out that sort of thing.'

'I don't think Detective Inspector Lloyd would like me getting involved,' said Lottie.

'Oh pfft to the detective!'

'Pfft indeed!' said Lady Buckley-Phipps. 'He's determined to punish our son because of the apple incident.'

'I feel sure that someone put a lot of planning into Percy Abercromby's murder,' said Lord Buckley-Phipps. 'And it's enormously inconvenient that they chose to do it under our roof!'

'Some people are terribly inconsiderate,' said his wife. 'Why couldn't they have done it elsewhere?'

'Because there was a useful weapon here, I suppose,' said Lord Buckley-Phipps.

'If only they hadn't found it! That letter opener should have been kept under lock and key.'

'They could just as easily taken a knife from the kitchen. You can't lock everything up, Lucinda.'

The Dowager Lady Buckley-Phipps entered the room. 'Good morning everyone,' she said. Her three dogs ran up to Rosie, sniffed her, then lost interest and returned to their mistress.

'What are you doing here, Mother?' said Lord Buckley-Phipps. 'You should be resting.'

'I don't like lying up in my room on my own, I feel like I'm missing out on everything.'

'But you're injured!'

'Yes, but I'm determined to be brave about it. And I think moving around a little helps.'

'If you say so, Mother. But I don't want the injury getting any worse.'

'I shall let you know if it gets worse, Ivan, and you can call the doctor.' The old lady made her way to a chair by the fireplace. 'How is everyone this morning?' she said once she'd made herself comfortable.

'Lucinda is wishing she'd never invited the Abercrombys to dinner,' said Lord Buckley-Phipps.

'I can understand that. But no one could have predicted something so terrible would happen.'

'Fate decided the two families wouldn't get along with each other,' said Lord Buckley-Phipps. 'This is what happens when you meddle with fate.'

'I didn't try to meddle with fate!' said Lady Buckley-Phipps. 'All I tried to do was heal a rift.'

'The road to hell is paved with good intentions, Lucinda. It's awfully tragic that Percy Abercromby was murdered in the library. But it's difficult to shed tears for a family who have made our lives miserable for the past three centuries.'

'Lucinda was doing her best, Ivan,' said the dowager. 'She did what she thought was right. The only person responsible for this atrocity is the murderer. The detective shouldn't be accusing Barty, he needs to hear my description of the culprit so he can look for him. Where can I find the detective?'

'He's been in the music room with Barty for over an hour now,' said Lord Buckley-Phipps. 'And he also spoke to him last night. Lucinda's getting fretful over it.'

'And so are you!' responded his wife.

'I shall have a word with him,' said the dowager, getting out of her chair.

'No, Mother, you must remain where you are. You need to recover from your fall.'

'The detective needs to leave Barty alone. I refuse to believe my grandson is to blame.' She made her way to the door. 'Where did you say they are? The music room?'

'Yes, but I don't think you should—'

'Oh, I'm fine Ivan. Please don't worry. I shall rescue Barty and ask the detective to look for the man who knocked me over.'

The elderly lady disappeared through the door and her dogs followed after her.

Chapter Twenty

'YOUR LADYSHIP?' Detective Inspector Lloyd got to his feet as the dowager entered the music room.

'Granny?' said Barty, also rising from his seat. 'What are you doing here? You should be—'

'Yes, I know I should be resting.'

She thought it was kind of her family to worry about her, but she felt the need to tell her story to the detective. She also needed to persuade him that Barty was incapable of committing murder.

'Have you finished talking to my grandson?' she asked. Her dogs yapped at the detective, then sniffed around his legs.

'Almost. It's important I get a detailed statement from him, my lady, because he was the last person to see Percy Abercromby alive.'

'No, he wasn't.'

'He wasn't?'

'No. The murderer was. And I absolutely refuse to believe my grandson would murder someone.'

'I'm afraid I must suspect everyone at this stage, my lady.'

'But you haven't even interviewed me yet. And I'm the one who saw the murderer!'

'I was told you needed time to recover from your ordeal, my lady.'

'I would like to tell you what I saw. Then you can get out there and search for the culprit. Barty needs a break from all this. It's been very upsetting for him and he's lost an old schoolfriend.'

The detective looked Barty up and down. 'Very well. As it is, I think we've gone over everything now.'

'Yes, we have,' said Barty wearily. 'Several times.'

'Go and take your mind off things, Barty,' said the dowager as she made her way to the table. 'The detective knows where to find you if he needs you again.'

'Thank you, Granny.'

She took a seat at the table, wincing a little as she felt some pain in her right hip from the fall.

The detective sat down again and puffed on his pipe as he gave himself time to think. Eventually, he picked up his notebook and pen. 'I'm delighted you've recovered enough to speak to me, my lady. Perhaps you can tell me how you came across the man who knocked you over?'

'I had been in the gardens walking my dogs. My son insisted we shut them in the gunroom during dinner because he says they can be a nuisance when there's food about. They're not actually a nuisance at all, but he wanted to create a good impression, I suppose. So as soon as dinner was over, I was keen to rescue my dogs and take them outside before it got dark.'

'Did you see anyone out in the gardens?'

'No.'

'There's been a report of a man loitering beneath an oak tree in the gardens at the front.'

'I didn't see him. I headed straight for the kitchen gardens, as I always do. I like it there. The area is walled, the paths are firm and there are some benches I like to rest on.'

'Did anyone see you there?'

'Let me think...' The dowager closed her eyes and tried to recall her walk. 'Yes, I did see someone there. Young Tilly the maid. She had finished her work for the evening and was probably getting some fresh air. We acknowledged each other and then went on our way. I don't know how long I was there. Perhaps twenty minutes. And when I returned to the house, that was when all the trouble started. I walked through the main entrance, into the entrance hall. Then I walked through to the saloon and I was heading for the drawing room where I knew the ladies had gathered after dinner and... whack! The man ran straight into me as he came out of the library. He knocked into my left shoulder and sent me crashing to the floor.'

'Did you see what he looked like?'

'Not at that point. The dogs had gone on ahead of me, you see, and my eyes were on them.'

'So then what happened?'

'Well, as soon as he knocked me, I remember toppling to my right. It all seemed to happen slowly. It's often the way when you have an accident, isn't it? For some reason, I had time to think about whether I could stop myself from falling. And by the time I'd decided I couldn't, the floor was coming up to meet me. My walking stick slipped from my hand and I tumbled onto my right side. I remember feeling pure indignation at the person who'd bumped into me. My immediate thought was that it was one of the servants, but I realise now they wouldn't have done such a thing.'

'So, did you see anything of him at all?'

'Only a little. When I was on the floor, I managed to turn my head and I just caught sight of him dashing into the entrance hall. It was the most fleeting of glimpses. He wore dark clothing and I think he had a cap on. I couldn't give you any more detail than that, I'm afraid. I worry if I try to dwell on the image of him too much, then I'm in danger of making up details.'

'It's very useful to get a description of him, my lady.'

'Well, I thought it would be. That's why I was surprised you hadn't spoken to me sooner. Anyway, I must add that when I was lying on the floor, I assumed the man who'd knocked me over was a burglar who had crept in, grabbed something from the library and made off with it. And it was at that point that I gathered my senses and called for help. People appeared from all directions and it was quite disorientating.'

'I understand Harry the footman was the first to reach you.'

'That's right, he was. A very helpful young man. I remember telling everyone I was fine and they had to get after the man who'd just run out of the door. I'm astonished no one caught up with him. And to think Barty was out there too and didn't see him, either. The man must have hidden somewhere. I suppose it was getting dark by then and it was easier to hide from view. You need to find him, Detective!'

'I'm doing my best.'

'I hope so. I was awfully shocked when I heard Percy Abercromby had been found dead in the library. I can't say I agreed with inviting the Abercrombys to dinner, but the young man didn't deserve such treatment.'

Chapter Twenty-One

LOTTIE TOOK Rosie for a walk in the gardens. It was another warm sunny day, and they came across the flower bed filled with lavender again. She watched the butterflies landing on the stalks of tiny purple flowers and Rosie scampered after a wood pigeon. It allowed her to get tantalisingly close before it lazily flapped away.

A bicycle appeared from around the corner of the house and turned into the servants' courtyard. It was the sort of bicycle a delivery boy would ride, with a large basket on the front. It had a squeak and Lottie was reminded of the person she'd seen leaving on a bicycle the previous evening. Could it be the same person?

She walked towards the house and called for Rosie to join her. As she passed the servants' courtyard, she saw Edward the footman smoking a cigarette. He was talking to the delivery boy, who had now dismounted. Lottie recognised him as the greengrocer's delivery boy, Tom Granger. She remembered him delivering fruit and vegetables to Fortescue Manor when she had worked as a maid. He was mousy-haired with narrow eyes and a wonky nose which looked like it had been broken.

Was it Tom Granger who she'd heard shout in anger the previous evening? She wondered who he'd been speaking to.

She passed the courtyard and went back into the house through a door at the rear. After passing through an alcove, she reached a corridor which passed the study. The door was closed, and she wondered if Lord Buckley-Phipps was inside. The study had been where the murder weapon had been kept. The murderer had presumably crept in there, taken the ornamental letter opener from the desk drawer, and hidden it in their clothing somehow. Lottie knew the study had two doors. One where she stood now in the corridor, and another which led to the morning room. Lottie wondered which door the murderer had used when they'd fetched the weapon.

She walked on. The corridor opened out into a small hallway with a staircase which was used by the family. A short corridor from the hallway led to the smoking room and the saloon. It wasn't a long walk from the study to the library, but the murderer had somehow managed it with no one noticing anything suspicious. An alternative route would have been to exit from the door at the back of the house and walk around the house to the front. But Lottie estimated that would take at least five minutes. Which way had the murderer gone? And surely someone would have seen them?

'Psst!'

The noise made Lottie startle. Mildred appeared from the doorway of the drawing room with a feather duster in her hand.

'I remembered something earlier,' she whispered. 'When Percy Abercromby was home from Cambridge at Easter time, he had a thing with a girl in the village.'

'Really?'

'Her name's Daisy Harris and she works at the biscuit factory. Percy stole her away from her boyfriend.'

'Oh dear, I can't imagine he was happy.'

'He wasn't. And you'll never guess who he is.'

'Who?'

'Harry Lewis.'

'The footman?'

Mildred giggled. 'Funny, isn't it? And to think that Percy Abercromby came to this house and Harry had to bow and scrape to him.'

'No wonder he was in a bad mood when he was serving dinner.'

'From what I hear, Daisy regrets it now because she and Harry were going steady for a while. Then Mr Abercromby came along and ruined it. I don't know what she saw in him, he wasn't very handsome, was he? I know it's wrong of me to say that, because he's no longer with us. But she must have been impressed by him because he was the son of a lord. Maybe she thought she was in with a chance of becoming a lady one day? That was never going to happen, though, was it? I suppose it all ended once she realised that. Apparently it broke Harry's heart.'

'So Harry must have been angry with Percy Abercromby.'

'Yes, he would have been. Oh no!' Mildred flung a palm to her cheek. 'You don't think that he...'

'Murdered Percy Abercromby in revenge?' said Lottie. 'It could explain why he was the first person on the scene when the Dowager Lady Buckley-Phipps was knocked over. Do you know Daisy?'

'Yes, I know her quite well. She's a friend of my cousin.'

'I expect she's upset about Percy's death.'

'She will be. Although the thing with him ended when he went back to university.'

'It would be helpful to speak to her and find out more.'

'That's a good idea! Let me think. I have the afternoon off tomorrow, perhaps we can wait for Daisy outside the biscuit factory and speak to her then?'

'That's a great idea, thank you.'

Mildred froze as they heard the jangle of keys on the housekeeper's belt as she walked along the corridor from the study. 'I'd better get on!' she whispered.

Chapter Twenty-Two

AFTER LEAVING Mildred to get on with her work, Lottie walked across the saloon to the library door. The door was ajar. She peered in at the room and wondered how the murderer had attacked Percy from behind. Presumably the assailant had crept up on him without him noticing.

'There you are, Lottie!' came Mrs Moore's voice from behind her. 'What have you been up to?'

'I've just taken Rosie out for a walk.'

Mrs Moore's face fell. 'Oh. I was going to ask if you'd like to accompany me on a stroll to the grotto. But I suppose you've probably tired yourself out.' She was wearing a plain dark dress and sensible walking shoes.

'No, I haven't worn myself out,' said Lottie. 'I'll come with you.'

'Oh good. Shall we go?'

They left the house by the door at the rear and followed a path to the right of the lake.

'Did peering in at the library give you any new ideas, Lottie?'

'It made me ponder how the murderer had crept up on Percy Abercromby from behind.'

'How do you know they did that?'

'Because he was stabbed in the back. I think that means he didn't see his attacker. Otherwise he would have attempted to fight them off, wouldn't he?'

'I hadn't even thought of that, Lottie! Of course he would. So the murderer must have been lying in wait for him in there. Hiding perhaps?'

'If they were hiding, that means they could have been in there when Barty and I were talking.' Lottie gave a shudder. 'That's not a nice thought.'

'No, it's not. But the murderer was after Percy, not you or Barty.'

They reached the rose garden where the dowager was stooped over some blooms. She wore a light overcoat, a wide sunhat and had a flower basket on one arm. 'Good morning!' she said. 'Is it still morning?'

'Just about, my lady,' said Mrs Moore. 'It's almost noon.'

'I thought so. The sun's probably at its highest point now, isn't it?' She squinted up at the sky. Her dogs ran over to Rosie, who stood as still as a statue until they'd finished sniffing her.

'Are you alright out here in the midday sun, my lady?' asked Mrs Moore.

'Oh yes, it's glorious out here.'

'It's just you had your fall—'

'Yes but I think the worst I can do is sit still and allow it to seize up. That's why I'm out here doing the dead-heading.'

'Of course, my lady,' said Mrs Moore. 'We shall leave you to it. We're on our way to the grotto.'

'Have a lovely walk!'

'We will. Thank you, my lady.'

'Astonishing isn't she?' said Mrs Moore, once they were

97

out of earshot. 'She's doing a spot of gardening when many ladies of her age are being pushed around in bath chairs. And after that fright she had last night too!'

Lottie's mind returned to the murderer hiding in the library. 'I suppose Harry Lewis, the footman, could be a suspect.'

'The footman? Are you thinking that because he was the one who found Percy in the library?'

'Also because he and Percy fell out over a girl called Daisy Harris.'

'Really?'

'Perhaps it's just gossip. But Mildred told me Daisy was courting Harry Lewis, and then Percy Abercromby stole her away. It was at Easter, apparently, when he was home from university. So the relationship with Harry Lewis ended and apparently he was very upset about it.'

'And who is Daisy Harris?'

'She's a friend of Mildred's cousin and works at the biscuit factory.'

'So Percy Abercromby was consorting with a commoner?'

'Apparently so.'

'I can't imagine Lord and Lady Abercromby being pleased about that. But I don't suppose they would have known about it.'

The path sloped downhill to where the little grotto was set in the hillside. Rosie trotted on ahead of them, sniffing the air and investigating the bases of tree trunks.

'So you think Harry Lewis could have been so upset about Daisy Harris that he murdered Percy Abercromby?' Mrs Moore asked Lottie.

'It's a possibility. Who knows what someone is capable of when they're extremely upset?'

'Indeed. Does the detective know about this?'

'I don't know. But I can't be sure enough about it yet to

mention it to him. Mildred has the afternoon off tomorrow so we're going to meet Daisy outside the biscuit factory and speak to her.'

Mrs Moore's eyes widened. 'Oh, that will be interesting! Daisy could have some useful information, couldn't she?'

They reached the arched cave-like entrance of the grotto.

'Oh, I do like this place,' said Mrs Moore, stepping inside. She peered at the interior through her lorgnette. 'It reminds me of an underwater cave! Not that I've ever been in an underwater cave. But I imagine this is what it would look like.'

Thousands of little shells decorated the curved walls. As Lottie's eyes adjusted to the gloom, she could see the patterns they'd been arranged in. The floor was patterned with little pebbles which felt bumpy beneath Lottie's feet. The air was cool and smelt of damp. As Mrs Moore ventured further into the grotto, Rosie remained by the entrance. The corgi seemed cautious about entering an enclosed space, and Lottie shared some of her trepidation. She recalled the servants telling each other ghost stories about the grotto. She didn't believe in ghosts, but the stories took on a new relevance as she stood inside the place.

'I like the little passageway at the back here,' said Mrs Moore from the echoey depths of the cave. 'I wish I'd brought a torch with me now, I don't think it's light enough to find my way and the floor's quite uneven, isn't it?'

Although the cave was pretty, Lottie wasn't keen on the damp and the gloom. She preferred to admire the decoration from the entrance where Rosie stood.

'I remember Lucinda telling me this grotto is very old,' said Mrs Moore. She was barely visible, but her voice echoed out into the sunshine. 'Eighteenth century, I think. Two hundred years! I'm amazed the shells are still stuck on the walls. It must have taken a very long time to stick them there.'

. . .

Once Mrs Moore had finished with the grotto, they walked back to the house.

'This is blowing the cobwebs away, isn't it, Lottie? It's just what we need. Although I'm rather puffed out. It's so peaceful here. It's difficult to believe something so terrible happened here yesterday evening, isn't it? And Detective Inspector Lloyd seems to have his sights set on poor Barty as the culprit. I refuse to believe he would have done such a thing. If you can find out more about Harry Lewis, then perhaps the detective will have a new suspect to consider.'

Chapter Twenty-Three

THE FOLLOWING AFTERNOON, Lottie and Mildred walked to the village of Lowton Chorley to catch a bus to Oswestry. The route took them down Hambledon Hill and Lottie enjoyed the view of the rolling hills in the sunshine. Birds tweeted in the hedgerows and bees buzzed around the oxeye daisies and rambling dog roses.

'It's nice to get out of the house, isn't it?' said Mildred. 'It's been miserable for the past few days. It's not surprising, I suppose. But it will be nice when everyone's in a better mood again. I don't mean that disrespectfully because it's not nice what happened, but...' she smiled. 'You know what I mean.'

'Yes I do,' said Lottie. Although Percy's death was a tragedy, no one at Fortescue Manor had known him well enough to mourn him.

Mildred lowered her voice, even though there was no one else around to hear. 'I've got some suspicions about the new maid, Tilly.'

Lottie startled. 'You think she could be a murderer?'

'No! Nothing that bad. But I think she might be stealing.'

'Oh no!'

'Last week, she took her apron off at the end of the day and a hair comb fell out of the apron pocket. She picked it up quickly and looked quite embarrassed about it. She told me she'd found it lying about and meant to return it to Lady Buckley-Phipps' room because she believed it belonged to her. It was a silver comb with jewels on it. The sort which her lady-ship wears in her hair. I was surprised that it would just be lying about. And I was also surprised she'd supposedly forgotten about returning it.'

'Perhaps she was telling the truth?'

'Maybe. But another time I found her with three silver teaspoons. She was in the drawing room at the time and said she'd left the dining room with them in her hand without real-ising. And then there was one afternoon when Mr Duxbury had gone down to the village and I saw her coming out of the butler's pantry.'

'Really?' Lottie was surprised at this because the butler's rooms were a place where no housemaid should venture.

'I asked her what she was doing there,' said Mildred. 'And she thought it was funny. She told me she'd dared herself to sneak into Mr Duxbury's rooms and have a look. She said his office and bedroom had been left unlocked. I told her she was silly and that she'd be in a lot of trouble if she got caught. And then I thought I should tell Mr Duxbury that he'd left his rooms unlocked, but then he would want to know how I knew it. Looking back now, I think Tilly was looking for something to take. And maybe she did take something? A nice pen from his desk perhaps, I don't know. But I'm sure she's up to no good. I don't have enough evidence that she's actually taking things, I just suspect it. And if she is taking things, then I suspect they're small things such as hair combs and silver teaspoons and she's hoping no one will notice.'

'She seems to be up to something, from what you say. But no one seems to have noticed anything missing yet.'

'Not yet. And I feel bad suspecting her because I know she's from a poor family. It can be difficult when you work in a house that's filled with lots of treasures and you come from a place with nothing.'

'Yes, it can be difficult,' said Lottie. 'But many servants come from poor backgrounds and we don't go about stealing. All you can do is keep an eye on her and if you actually see her take something, then you'll have to tell someone. If you merely suspect it, then there's not a lot you can do at the moment.'

The bus journey into Oswestry took about fifteen minutes. Mildred chatted along the way and Rosie sat on Lottie's lap and looked out of the window. As the bus entered Oswestry, it passed the red brick orphanage which had once been Lottie's home. She felt her heart skip a beat as her eyes lingered on the building. It was a place so familiar to her, and yet it no longer played a part in her life. The dowager's words replayed in her mind, *do you ever wonder who your parents were, Miss Sprigg?*

It was something many people had asked her over the years. And it was something she thought about a lot. But would she ever discover who they were?

Chapter Twenty-Four

Oswestry biscuit factory was a new brick building close to the railway line. As Lottie and Mildred approached, a pleasant, sweet baking smell lingered in the air.

They waited by the large gates and peered at the factory on the far side of the courtyard.

'Do you ever feel tempted to work here, Mildred?' Lottie asked.

'Me? No. I think I would get bored doing the same thing over and over. I know the money and hours are better, but I like working in service. I feel like I'm part of something at Fortescue Manor. Part of a family, I suppose.' She smiled. 'And no day is ever the same. There's always something happening, isn't there?'

'There certainly seems to be.'

A siren sounded and a man in overalls opened the tall gates. Moments later, a crowd of workers traipsed across the courtyard and spilled out onto the street. Lottie could see people of all ages. Many were chatting and laughing and were pleased to have finished their work for the day.

Lottie wondered how easy it was going to be to spot Daisy Harris in the crowd.

'Oh, I think that's her!' said Mildred. She stood on her tiptoes as workers streamed past. 'Oh, hang on... no, it's not.'

A few people stopped to pat Rosie on the head and the corgi's tail wagged excitedly as she greeted everyone.

'I think that's her!' said Mildred. 'The one with the bonnet... no, it's not.'

The crowd thinned and Lottie wondered if they'd missed Daisy completely. It would have been quite easy to miss her in the crowd.

Then Mildred grabbed Lottie's arm. 'Now that's her, there! What's she doing speaking to Ruthie Prior? I didn't think she liked her. Anyway, come on, let's speak to her.'

Mildred pulled Lottie through the crowd to an attractive, freckle-faced young woman.

'Hello Daisy!'

'Mildred! This is a surprise. How are you?' Her companion, Ruthie, said goodbye and went on her way.

'I'm fine. This is Miss Sprigg, we used to work together at Fortescue Manor, but she's a travelling companion now to Lady Buckley-Phipps' sister.'

Daisy Harris gave an impressed smile. 'Have you travelled to lots of places, Miss Sprigg?'

'She's travelled all round the world!' said Mildred.

'Not quite around the world. Just some places in Europe. And Cairo.'

'You've been to Egypt, Miss Sprigg?'

'Yes. And it was fascinating. But please call me Lottie.'

'Let's find somewhere for a chat,' said Mildred, glancing around. 'How about the bench by the duck pond?'

Lottie recalled walks to the duck pond when she was a girl. It had been a treat for the orphans to go there and feed the ducks. Today some ducks were resting on their little island in the centre of the pond. Rosie eyed them and seemed disappointed she could get nowhere near.

'What's this about?' asked Daisy as they sat down.

'Percy Abercromby,' said Mildred.

'Oh.' Daisy pulled a handkerchief from her sleeve and wiped her eyes.

'You must be very upset,' said Mildred.

'A little bit. We were together for a short while but then he told me he didn't want to see me anymore. So I was feeling angry about him before he died. I'd decided I didn't like him anymore because of the way he treated me, but I was shocked when I heard he'd been murdered. And a bit upset too, even though I didn't like him in that way anymore. But I'd liked him a lot once and so I felt sad for him. He didn't deserve it.'

'Do you know if he'd upset anyone?' Lottie asked.

'I think he probably upset a few people.'

'Like Harry?' said Mildred.

'I suppose Harry was upset when I left him for Percy.'

'He was very upset!'

'Oh don't say that, it makes me feel awful about it.'

'I blame Percy,' said Mildred. 'He swept you off your feet because he's the son of a lord.'

'Yes, I suppose that had something to do with it. But I'm to blame too.'

'Do you think Harry could have murdered Percy?' said Mildred.

'No!'

'But he was the one who found him.'

'He wouldn't do something like that. You think he murdered him over me?'

'It could have been revenge,' said Mildred.

'No! I'm really not someone who people would murder each other over. Harry wouldn't have done that. Do the police suspect him?'

'I don't know,' said Lottie.

'I hope they don't. Harry isn't perfect, he... oh, I'm not saying anything more. It's really none of my business what he does these days.'

'What are you talking about, Daisy?' asked Mildred.

'It's not my business anymore, like I say.'

'Presumably you got to know Percy Abercromby quite well?' Lottie asked.

'Fairly well. It only lasted about a month, and I was never invited to Clarendon Park. I'm not the sort of girl he would introduce to his parents! I think he was a disappointment to his father, though.'

'Why do you say that?'

'Because he didn't want to do the things which his father wanted him to do. He much preferred books, and he was very knowledgeable about a lot of different things. He would talk about them a lot and I would listen, but it went over my head most of the time. I can see now that we didn't really have anything in common. I was impressed by him because of who he was. It was silly really, I should have stayed with Harry.'

'You mentioned Percy upset a few people,' said Lottie. 'Who else did he upset apart from Harry?'

'I remember he had an argument with the greengrocer.'

'Mr Harcourt?' said Mildred.

'Yes. We were in Lowton Chorley and we went into the greengrocers, because he wanted to buy some grapes. Percy complained the grapes were mouldy, and he told Mr Harcourt he would only pay half price for them. I don't understand why because they looked fine to me. Mr Harcourt refused and Percy got annoyed and accused him of selling mouldy fruit and vegetables. Then he told him he was going to ask his family to change their supplier. And can you believe it, he did! And so Clarendon Park changed their supplier and I've heard Mr Harcourt lost a lot of business from it.'

'What a horrible thing for Percy to do!' said Mildred. 'Mr Harcourt must have been very upset.'

'He must have been. And all because Percy wanted to pay less for the grapes. I should have realised then that I'd made a mistake. Someone that rich trying to pay half the price for something! It was very rude of him.'

'Well Harcourt is still the supplier for Fortescue Manor and I've never known any of his fruit and vegetables to be mouldy,' said Mildred. 'And although Harcourt must have been angry with Percy, he can't possibly have murdered him because he wasn't at Fortescue Manor on the night Percy was murdered.'

'Not that we know of,' said Lottie. 'But maybe he sneaked his way in?'

'How would he have done that?'

'I don't know.' Lottie thought of Harcourt's delivery boy and the cyclist she'd seen leaving late that evening. 'I need to have a think.'

Chapter Twenty-Five

BARTY WANDERED down Hambledon Hill with his hands in his pockets. He felt glum. He'd been in many scrapes during his life, but nothing as serious as this! He felt sure that the more he tried to plead his innocence to Detective Inspector Lloyd, the more guilty he appeared.

A horse and rider were trotting up the hill towards him. As they drew nearer, he realised with horror that the rider was Evelyn. He felt his heart thud and his face heat up. He had no idea what to say to Evelyn. Did she think he'd murdered her brother? Was he about to endure a confrontation? A barrage of angry words, perhaps?

He glanced about him, wondering if he could hide some-where. The steep banks of the lane rose either side of him and the only refuge was a prickly hawthorn bush.

He had to speak to her.

Evelyn slowed her horse to a walk, and Barty prepared himself for the interaction.

'Hello, Barty,' she said as she brought the horse to a halt. Did he detect anger in her voice? He couldn't be sure. The horse was grey and a good size. Evelyn towered over him and was as beautiful as he remembered her on the evening of the dinner. And now she was going to shout at him and call him horrible names about murdering her brother. He decided to offer her his condolences before the expected onslaught began.

'Hello Evelyn. I'm very sorry about Percy.'

'Thank you, Barty, that's kind of you.'

A pause followed as she presumably mustered the energy to shout at him.

But everything remained quiet, and Barty felt the need to say something more. 'I knew him for a long time,' he added. 'We were at school together.'

'That's right.' She smiled.

The encounter was going far better than he'd hoped, so he spoke some more. 'We weren't close at school,' he continued. 'But I always found Percy quite entertaining, he was never dull, that's for sure.'

'Oh, he was dull.'

'Was he?' He looked up at her, surprised by her words.

'You don't have to say nice things about him,' she said. 'I know the pair of you didn't get on with each other. And that was to be expected because of the feud between our families. I loved my brother very much and I miss him enormously. But I shan't pretend he was everyone's cup of tea, because he wasn't.'

'You're comparing your late brother to a cup of tea?'

'Yes. A cup of tea that was too strong or too weak for people. Depending on how you like your tea.'

'Quite strong for me.'

'Me too. So there's no need to pretend you liked him, because I know that's not true.'

'I didn't murder him, if that's what you're thinking.'

'I don't think you murdered him.'

'But your parents do.'

'They're shocked and upset. They're desperate to blame your family. I think they'll change their minds about you once they've had time to consider it.'

'I hope so. But Detective Inspector Lloyd thinks I did it too. I'm going to be arrested, I just know it.'

'But they can't charge you without any evidence.'

'And what if no evidence is found at all? Then they'll just charge me because I happened to have been the one most likely to have done it.'

'They can't do that.'

'I hope not. And I hope for your sake, Evelyn, that they find the person who did this to your brother. You're right in saying I didn't like him very much. He didn't like me very much, either. But I feel awfully sad he's dead. I never would have thought such a thing could happen to him.'

'Me neither.'

'So how are you keeping?' he asked. 'That sounds like a silly question because of what's happened, but I hope you're keeping as well as can be.'

'I am. Thank you Barty. My mother didn't want me to come out riding, but it's rather miserable at home at the moment. We're all in mourning. I prefer to remember my brother while out in the beautiful countryside rather than cooped up at home.'

'I think that's a wonderful way of remembering someone.'

'You do?'

'Yes. Moping around all day in a chair isn't going to solve anything, is it?'

'I don't believe so.' The horse tossed its head, as if impatient to move. 'I should get on. It's been nice seeing you again, Barty.'

'Has it?' It surprised him she would say such a thing.

111

'Yes.' She smiled. 'Enjoy your walk.'

'And you enjoy yours. Although I suppose it's the horse which is doing the walking, rather than you. I should have said ride instead of walk, shouldn't I?'

'Bye Barty!' She rode off at a trot, and Barty admonished himself for talking nonsense.

Chapter Twenty-Six

LOTTIE FOUND Mrs Moore in the sitting room before dinner. She was reading a fashion magazine.

'There you are, Lottie! How did you get on with the factory girl?'

Lottie told her about the meeting with Daisy Harris.

'She doesn't think Harry the footman could be the murderer?' said Mrs Moore in a whisper.

'No. But she told me something interesting about Mr Harcourt the greengrocer.' Lottie told her about the accusation of mouldy grapes and the greengrocer being dropped as a supplier to Clarendon Park.

'Oh golly,' said Mrs Moore. 'Poor Mr Harcourt.'

'I think either Mr Harcourt or his delivery boy Tom Granger were here at the house that night. When I was out walking Rosie, I saw someone go off on a bicycle. And before that, I'd heard someone raise their voice in the servants' courtyard.'

'What did they say?'

'I didn't catch the words, but they sounded angry. And yesterday I saw Tom Granger arrive at the house. He cycled into the courtyard and the bicycle squeaked, just the same as the bicycle I'd seen the previous evening.'

'A lot of bicycles squeak, Lottie.'

'It sounded like the same type of squeak. Regular as if it came from a wheel or a pedal.'

'So you think it was the same bicycle on both occasions?'

'Yes. And now I've learned about the incident with the mouldy grapes, I'm wondering if Mr Harcourt or Tom Granger sneaked into the house to attack Percy Abercromby. One of them could have hidden in the library, couldn't they?'

'I suppose so. But I don't see how they could have walked around the house without someone noticing,' said Mrs Moore.

'Perhaps it was Tom? He's a delivery boy so people are accustomed to seeing him here.'

'But only in or near the servants' quarters. He wouldn't be in the main part of the house, would he?'

'No. But perhaps he succeeded in hiding in the library with no one seeing him make his way there.'

'It can't be ruled out, I suppose. But how would he have known Percy would be in the library?'

'Perhaps he was watching from somewhere? Or overheard a conversation?'

'Lurking about, listening in?' said Mrs Moore. 'What a horrible thought!'

'Or someone told him?'

'Who?'

'Perhaps he was tipped off by one of the servants who overheard the conversation at dinner.'

'So there could be more than one person involved?' said Mrs Moore.

'It's possible, isn't it? I think I'm complicating it now. I shall ask Mr Harcourt about Percy and the grapes. I'd like to determine if it's a true story.'

'That's an excellent idea, Lottie. It's important to verify what someone's told you. After all, they could be telling you any old story just to suit their own circumstances, couldn't they?'

Mr Duxbury entered the room and presented Mrs Moore with an envelope. 'A letter for you in this evening's post, Mrs Moore.'

'Thank you, Duxbury.'

He left the room, and she examined the writing on the envelope. 'Oh no,' she groaned. 'This looks like another letter from Bertrand Sykes. Dare I even open it?'

Before Lottie could reply, her employer was ripping open the envelope. She pulled out the letter and read aloud. '"My dear Roberta." I wish he wouldn't call me that. I'm Mrs Moore to him. "My dear sister, Joanne, and I are mortified to hear about the terrible tragedy at Fortescue Manor. You and your family must be extremely distressed by the incident and Joanne and I send you our thoughts and prayers. Perhaps, at this difficult time, you are in need of somewhere peaceful to stay? If so, then you are most welcome to visit us and stay for as long as you wish. I shan't be returning to London until September. If there is anything else we can do for you, then please don't hesitate to ask. I remain your loyal friend, Bertrand Sykes."'

Mrs Moore sighed. 'He makes himself sound friendly and pleasant, doesn't he? But if I only had a cent to my name, he wouldn't be writing me letters. I suppose it was rather remiss of me not to reply to his previous letter.'

'You shouldn't have to if you don't want to.'

'True, Lottie. It's not good manners, but neither is pursuing someone because you want to marry them for their wealth.'

The Dowager Lady Buckley-Phipps entered the room.

Rosie's ears lowered as the three dogs inspected her. When they left, Rosie sat on Lottie's feet for reassurance.

'Good afternoon, my lady,' said Mrs Moore.

'Good afternoon.' The dowager settled into a chair. 'Have you heard if the detective has caught that murderer yet?'

'Not to my knowledge.'

'What a shame.' The dowager shook her head. 'I worry they're going to get away with it. What's that you have in your hand?'

'A letter from somebody I don't wish to hear from.'

'Oh dear, what a nuisance.'

'So I'm going to toss it away if that's alright.'

'Do go ahead,' said the dowager.

Mrs Moore scrunched the letter into a ball and threw it at the wastepaper basket. But before it could get there, one of the dowager's dogs leapt up, snatched the paper ball out of the air and ran around the room with it in its mouth.

'Oh, drop that, Lord Byron,' said the dowager. 'It's intended for the bin!'

The dog did so. But then another dog got hold of it and began pulling it to pieces.

'Wordsworth!' said the dowager. 'Don't make a mess!'

But the ball of paper was soon in shreds all over the carpet.

'Oh goodness,' sighed the dowager. She rang the bell for the maid.

Chapter Twenty-Seven

LOTTIE AND ROSIE walked into Lowton Chorley the following day. The cobbled high street was busy with people shopping, running errands and pausing to chat with each other. Colourful shop awnings provided some shade from the sun. Rosie greeted some of the local dogs and inspected each lamppost. Harcourt's greengrocer shop occupied a prominent spot. Crates of vegetables were displayed outside: shiny red tomatoes, plump cucumbers and carrots with leafy green tops.

Lottie asked Rosie to wait outside the shop for her and went inside. She picked up three apples and took them over to the counter where Mr Harcourt stood. He was a broad man with steely eyes. A cap was perched on his bald head, and a green and white striped apron covered his broad girth.

'I recognise you, don't I?' he said as he placed Lottie's apples into a paper bag. 'You work at Fortescue Manor, but I've not seen you for a while.'

'That's because I've been away. I'm employed as a travelling companion for Mrs Moore, she's Lady Buckley-Phipps' sister.'

'I've come across her before. Talkative lady.'

'Sometimes.'

'That will be threepence.' He held out his large hand for the money. His fingers were like thick sausages.

'It's been rather strange at Fortescue Manor for the past few days,' said Lottie, as she placed her coin on his palm. 'No one expected a murder to happen.' She hoped her words might prompt him to say something about Percy Abercromby.

'It's most unfortunate indeed.' He dropped the coin into his cash register and closed it with a slam.

'I don't know if this story is true or not,' she ventured, 'but I heard Percy Abercromby came in here and complained about your produce.'

'Oh, you heard about that, did you?' He took off his cap, scratched his head, then replaced the cap again. 'Yes, that was a few months ago. I know I shouldn't speak ill of him, but that young man had a pompous attitude. And, as a result, they dropped me as a supplier to Clarendon Park. It was a big blow at the time because I lost a lot of income.' He lowered his voice. 'I shouldn't be talking about it, really.'

'Why not?'

'Because people talk! Once Detective Inspector Lloyd learns I had a gripe with Percy Abercromby, then he's going to come knocking at my door, isn't he? And I really don't welcome that.'

'He can't possibly think you were responsible for Percy's death, can he?'

'Who knows what he thinks? All I know is you have to be careful at times like this. For as long as that murderer is on the run, any of us could be a suspect. Let's just hope that detective hurries up and catches him. And in the meantime, I won't be drawn on my opinion of young Mr Abercromby. May his soul rest in peace.'

'Of course,' said Lottie. 'May I ask one more question?'

'You may, but I can't promise to answer it.'

'Do you do evening deliveries?'

He frowned. 'Evening deliveries? No.'

'What's the latest time your delivery boy goes out?'

'Now you're asking me two questions. Why?'

'I'm just wondering.'

'The deliveries stop when the shop closes. And the shop closes at half-past five every day, Monday to Saturday.'

'Alright then. Thank you for the apples, Mr Harcourt.'

Chapter Twenty-Eight

LOTTIE WENT to her room when she returned to Fortescue Manor. She sat on her bed with Rosie and opened her notebook. There was a lot to write, and she wanted to make sure she didn't forget anything. As she wrote, she reflected on her conversation with Mr Harcourt. Although he'd been polite, his manner had seemed brusque. And he'd also seemed wary of saying too much about Percy Abercromby. Did he have something to hide?

Lottie noticed she'd written a reminder in her notebook. She was supposed to be writing to everyone she'd made friends with on her travels. She'd promised them letters and yet she'd written nothing. Percy's murder had distracted her. After making some notes, she got out her letter writing set.

There was a knock at her door and Mildred and Tilly stepped in.

'Oh, here you are, Lottie! We've got something to tell you, but we need to be quick before Mrs Hudson catches us. Tilly's got something to tell you about Harry.'

'What's that?'

Tilly stepped forward. She was a slender girl with prominent ears. 'I was just telling Mildred that I think Harry Lewis is up to something. I thought it before the murder and I still think it now.'

'Why?'

'He goes out at night. I see him from my window. I like to look out at the stars before I go to bed and that's when I see him.'

'Tilly says he goes past the lake and over to the hedgerow.'

'There's a path through there?'

'There must be,' said Mildred.

'But beyond the hedgerow, there's the hilly field,' said Lottie. 'So why does he go there?'

'There's the road at the top of the field.'

'You think he goes that far?'

'He might do. And Tilly's got an idea, haven't you Tilly?'

'Yes. I think he crosses the road to get to Clarendon Park.'

Lottie knew the boundary of Clarendon Park lay on the other side of the road. 'Why would he do that?'

Both maids shrugged.

'Have you asked Harry about it?'

'No!' They shook their heads.

'I don't want Harry thinking I'm spying on him,' said Tilly.

'And if he's up to no good, then he might threaten us with something,' added Mildred. 'There's no way I'm mentioning it to him. It's a mystery. But I told Tilly we should let you know because we're a bit suspicious of Harry, aren't we?'

'I suppose we are,' said Lottie. 'There's only one way of finding out what he's up to. And that's to follow him.'

'I'm not following him!' said Tilly. 'I don't like being out in the dark.'

Mildred bit her lip. 'I'll go if you need help, Lottie.'

'Do you want to?'

'Not really. Like Tilly, I'm not keen on the dark. But you shouldn't follow him on your own.'

'Shall we go this evening?'

'Alright then. Let's go this evening.' She eyed Lottie's letter writing set. 'What are you writing?'

'I have to catch up on my correspondence,' said Lottie. 'I made some friends on my travels who I need to write to. I promised each of them I'd stay in touch.'

'Who are they?'

'Stefano in Venice, Pierre in Paris, Karim in Cairo, Henri in Monaco and Josef in Vienna.'

Mildred laughed. 'All boys?'

'Yes, but it's not what you think. They're just friends.'

Mildred laughed again and nudged Tilly with her elbow. 'Now we know what Lottie was really doing on her travels!' The pair giggled.

Lottie smiled. 'Each of them helped me.'

'How?'

'Well, it was quite strange, but there happened to be a murder in each place we stayed in.'

'Oh no, Lottie, how shocking!'

'Yes, it was. But each case was solved and my friends helped.'

Mildred shook her head. 'That's why I never want to travel anywhere. It's much too dangerous!'

Chapter Twenty-Nine

THE DOWAGER LADY Buckley-Phipps snipped off the wilted rose heads and kept an eye out for some nice blooms she could put in a vase.

'Hello Granny!'

It was Barty. She stood up, wincing at the pain in her back from stooping.

'You're looking a bit brighter today, Barty. Is the detective leaving you alone now?'

'He is, for the time being.' He patted the three dogs who greeted him, tails wagging. 'Although I'm worried he might pounce on me again.'

'Well, if he does, I shall tell him to leave you alone. I know you wouldn't have harmed that young man.'

'Thank you, Granny. Although I really should learn to stand on my own two feet now. There can't be many chaps my age who have their grandmother helping out.'

'I'll do what I can while I'm still around. Our family and this place are precious to me.' She gave the house a fond glance. Its walls were glowing a warm cream in the sunshine. 'I remember arriving here as a young bride. I was raised in Hertfordshire and had never been to Shropshire before. I fell in love with the place immediately. We had more staff back then, and they were more respectful and loyal, too. No one would have ever left to work in a biscuit factory. Generations of families worked as servants at Fortescue Manor. They were born here, then they lived, worked and died within the estate walls. Many of them are buried in the chapel graveyard.'

'They must have been very dedicated.'

'They were! They knew they were lucky to work for our family. And we had a lot of work to do, this house badly needed repair when we took it over. When I married into the Buckley-Phipps family, I hadn't realised the extent of their financial problems. My father-in-law died, leaving nothing in his will. Your grandfather inherited a crumbling estate. So we had to forge a plan for your father. We found some funds to send him off to America and socialise with the wealthy families on the east coast. That was how he met your mother, the daughter of a railroad tycoon. She didn't have the ancient bloodline which was traditionally required for this family, but she did have lots of money.'

'Good old Mother.'

'Fortunately for us, she fell in love with your father and with Fortescue Manor. She worked hard to restore the house to its former glory.'

'And I'm glad she did.'

'But life is getting harder again now, Barty. Things have changed since the war. Taxes are increasing and fewer people want to work in service. Many of them, especially women, are choosing to work elsewhere. In secretarial jobs, in factories and so on. You have a challenge ahead of you.'

'I suppose I do. I don't like to dwell on it too much. After all, Father is still young and lively so he'll be around for a long time yet.'

'He's not as young and lively as he was, Barty. And life is

full of surprises. A sudden death can befall anyone, can't it? Just look at poor young Percy Abercromby.'

'I don't like to think of such things happening in our family, Granny!'

'Neither do I. But we mustn't ignore such possibilities. I've been blessed to have led such a long life and I can only hope my descendants enjoy the same. I say, who's that!'

The figure of a man appeared on the slope which led down to the grotto. But as soon as she spotted him, he ducked away again.

'Who?' Barty spun around. He hadn't seen him.

'I saw a man, just there!' She pointed.

'Are you sure?'

'Of course I'm sure! He was as clear as you are to me now, Barty.'

Her grandson strode over to the spot she'd pointed out and looked around. 'No sign of him!' he called back.

The dowager felt sure about what she'd seen. 'I didn't imagine it, Barty. He was there!'

Chapter Thirty

THE KNOCK on Lottie's door came just after midnight. It was Mildred.

'I've just seen Harry head down to the lake!' she whispered excitedly.

'Let's go!'

They crept along the corridor, their shoes in their hands. Then they dashed down the service staircase and left by the kitchen and servants' courtyard. Rosie trotted with them, no doubt intrigued by the night-time excursion.

Outside, the lawns were grey in the moonlight and the lake was a large black expanse. 'Tilly says he goes past the lake to the hedgerow,' whispered Mildred. 'Let's head that way and if we run fast enough, hopefully we'll catch sight of him.'

The night was calm and still. Rosie appeared to have picked up Harry's scent and scampered ahead of them. The moon lit their way, and they soon reached the dark shape of the hedgerow.

'Tilly says he goes through here,' said Mildred. 'There has to be a gap somewhere.'

They paced up and down it, looking for a way through.

'Here!' said Lottie.

'Well done!'

They dashed along a narrow dark path, through shrubbery which pulled at Lottie's sleeves and skirt. Eventually, they came out into a meadow which sloped up to the boundary wall. It was easy to see where the long grass had been trodden, so they followed the route.

Lottie caught sight of movement at the top of the slope.

'Is that him?' she whispered.

'Yes! It must be. He's by the wall, I think.'

They ran up through the meadow, the long grass whipping at their legs. Rosie bounded alongside, clearly enjoying the run.

Lottie could see a figure clambering over the wall, then Harry disappeared. He'd presumably dropped down onto the road.

They reached the top of the slope about a minute later, puffing and panting. The craggy stone wall was about five feet high. An old tree stump had been placed at the base of the wall. 'This must be how he gets over,' whispered Mildred.

Mildred clambered over first, and Lottie handed Rosie to her before she followed. The rough stone grazed her palms and knees as she went.

They were on the road now. Lottie glanced up and down it. It wound away either side of them like a long grey ribbon.

'There's no sign of Harry,' she said. 'He must have climbed the wall into Clarendon Park.' She glanced at the wall on the other side of the road, it was much taller than the wall they'd just climbed over.

'How did he get over that?' said Mildred.

They walked over to it and Lottie felt the rough stone. 'He must have found some footholds somewhere.'

'Maybe he's just really good at climbing,' said Mildred. 'But I'm not. And now we can't follow him anymore!'

Lottie glanced around and realised Rosie was nowhere to be seen. Just moments previously, she had seen the dog's shadowy form close by. But now she'd vanished.

'Rosie!' she called out.

All of a sudden, the dog emerged from the wall.

'Where did you get to?' Lottie asked. Then she peered at the wall. 'Just a moment,' she said. 'I think there's a gap we can crawl through!'

'Brilliant!'

'Rosie just found it for us.'

Lottie crouched down and saw the moonlit field on the other side of the wall. 'I think we can just about get through there.'

'If Harry can, then we certainly can!'

They had to lower themselves to their stomachs and wiggle through, but moments later, they were in the field belonging to Clarendon Park. It sloped down to some woodland at the bottom. Lottie felt her stomach tighten now she was in a place she wasn't supposed to be.

'I think the house is on the other side of the trees,' said Mildred.

Lottie glanced around. 'Is there anywhere else he could have gone?'

'It's difficult to say. But let's assume he's going to the house.'

'There!' Lottie pointed at movement by the trees.

'Let's go!'

Following Rosie, they made their way across the moonlit field. The grass was short and grazed, and Lottie could see dark outlines of cows huddled in the distance.

They reached the woodland and followed Rosie along a

little narrow path. It was dark with moonlight only occasionally reaching through the thick canopy overhead.

Eventually, the woodland thinned and the dark outline of Clarendon Park loomed into view.

'Where could he have gone?' whispered Mildred. The house was in darkness.

'It's very mysterious.'

They stepped out of the woods and kept close to the trees as they skirted the edge of the gardens.

'Over there!' whispered Mildred. She pointed at a yellow light. 'I think that's the stable block.'

They crept closer, and the light grew brighter. Lottie could see now that it was a light in the window.

'I can hear voices now,' said Mildred.

Lottie could hear them, too. It sounded like a group of young men.

They stopped by the trees.

'I'm owed three pounds, I tell you!'

'It's not three pounds. It's not even a pound. What do you say, Harry?'

'Let's make it a pound.'

'A pound? It's less than that.'

'It's not. It's three!'

Lottie crept across the grass towards the stable block. The window was open, and she caught a whiff of cigarette smoke. She could see saddles stored on the wall of the room.

'I'm not leaving here until I get my three pounds!'

'Then you're in for a long night.'

Lottie and Rosie stopped a few yards from the window. She felt confident that the light in the tack room was too bright for the room's occupants to see outside.

She could see a young man standing up. He wasn't anyone she recognised. He was addressing the other two as though they were both sat down.

'If you're not going to give me my three pounds, then I'll fetch someone who can help me.'

'Are you threatening us, William?'

Then the young man on his feet glanced at the window. He frowned, then said, 'I think someone's out there.'

Chapter Thirty-One

LOTTIE'S HEART leapt into her mouth. She turned and ran back to the trees as quickly as she could.

But Rosie didn't follow.

'Rosie!' Lottie hissed.

But the dog ignored her. A door had opened at the side of the building and the dog was presumably excited about greeting whoever stepped out of it.

Lottie's heartbeat thudded in her ears.

'They saw you?' asked Mildred.

'I think so.'

'Oh no!' They stepped further back into the trees. Lottie could do nothing about Rosie now. If she tried to fetch her back, she would give herself away.

A dark figure appeared. 'There's a dog,' he said. It sounded like Harry.

Rosie decided she didn't wish to be friendly with him and ran back towards Lottie and Mildred. Although Lottie was pleased to have her back, she knew now that Rosie had given away their position.

The figure strode towards the trees. 'Who's here?' he said.

The other two men joined him.

'There was a dog out here just now and it's just run into those trees. There must be someone there.'

'We need to run!' whispered Mildred.

'We can't, they'll hear our every move.'

'We have to go!'

'No. They'll hear us. Just duck down and keep still.'

They lowered themselves into the undergrowth as a torch was switched on. Its beam swept over the tree trunks in front of them. Rosie sat quietly with them. Lottie carefully shielded the dog's face with her hand, knowing Rosie's eyes would shine brightly if captured in the torchlight.

Another torch was switched on and Lottie huddled down, holding her breath.

Mildred was still and silent next to her.

'Are you sure there's someone here?' said a voice.

'I thought I saw someone through the window,' said another.

'And there was a dog out here just now,' said Harry.

'Sure you're not seeing things?'

'No! There's someone here.'

Lottie held her breath and prayed the young men would return to the stable block.

'If there was someone, they must've gone now.'

'But what if they saw what we were doing? They might tell someone.'

'We could let the dogs out. They'll soon find them.'

Lottie felt her blood run cold. Mildred gave a whimper. The dogs would find them quickly. And she didn't fancy encountering them either, they were probably trained to attack intruders.

'Well, if there's someone on the estate, then we should let the dogs out. We can tell Lord Abercromby that we heard a noise and got suspicious.'

The torch beams criss-crossed the woods.

Lottie trembled. It had been a mistake following Harry here.

She had to stop them from letting the dogs out. So the best thing she could do was create a distraction.

She whispered her plan into Mildred's ear.

'Will it work?'

'It has to. Just stay where you are until I say run.'

Lottie felt about on the ground. The earth was damp and finally her fingers found a stone. Slowly, she raised her arm.

'I'll go and get the dogs,' said someone.

Now was Lottie's chance. She flung the stone as far as she could to her right. She heard it hit a trunk and land in the undergrowth.

'What was that?' shouted one of the men. They dashed over to where the stone had landed, torchlights flashing. Fortunately, it was about twenty yards from Lottie, Rosie and Mildred.

'Let's go,' Lottie whispered. 'But move carefully, we don't want them to hear us.'

Someone was crashing about in the undergrowth where the stone had fallen. Lottie, Rosie and Mildred took advantage of the noise to quietly make their getaway.

'I can't see anyone!' came the cry behind them.

Once they were out of the woods, they began to run across the field of cows and up to the wall. The uphill dash was hard, and Lottie could feel the muscles in her legs burning with the strain.

They were halfway up the field when the baying of dogs sounded behind them.

'Oh no!' shrieked Mildred. 'They're after us!'

'Just run!' shouted Lottie. 'As fast as you can!'

Rosie ran the fastest, and they were able to follow her bounding form across the grass.

But the barking dogs were quickly gaining on them.

Lottie's lungs were sore from the deep breaths she needed to keep moving. Her legs stumbled as the pain intensified.

The wall still seemed so far away.

The dogs were out in the field now and catching up with them fast.

'Oh help!' cried Mildred. 'They're going to get us!'

'Don't talk!' said Lottie. 'Save your energy.'

Mildred was tiring and dropping behind.

'We're nearly there!'

She kept her eyes fixed on Rosie ahead, the dog knew where the hole in the wall was.

Finally, the wall was close but Mildred had slowed.

Lottie reached the wall and turned to see Mildred about thirty yards behind her. Just beyond her were the dark shapes of three barking dogs. Lottie felt sick with worry. Would Mildred be able to make it?

Rosie dashed through the hole and Lottie hoped it was too small for the Clarendon Park dogs to get through. It wouldn't take her long to duck and crawl to safety, but she didn't want to leave Mildred on her own in the field with the dogs.

'Quick Mildred!' she cried out. 'You can get away!'

She ran back to her and took her hand. Mildred whimpered and sobbed as Lottie pulled her up the final few yards.

'Get through the hole!' Lottie cried out. The dogs were close enough for her to see the glint of their eyes and teeth.

Mildred crawled through the hole and Lottie dropped to the ground and crawled after her. As she went, one of the dogs gripped the heel of her shoe. She pulled, and the dog pulled. For a moment she was stuck, and fearful that the other dogs would set themselves on her. But her shoe came loose, and she scrambled free.

Across the road, Mildred was already on top of the other wall.

'I've already put Rosie over,' she called out. 'Run Lottie!'

Lottie scrambled across the road. The dogs behind her paused for a moment, as if wondering whether they should leave their territory. Then one ran out into the road just as she was scaling the boundary wall of Fortescue Manor.

Mildred grabbed Lottie's arms and hauled her over as the dog barked at the base of the wall.

They fell into the field in a heap, gasping for breath.

Chapter Thirty-Two

EVERYONE GATHERED in the drawing room the following morning to hear an update from Detective Inspector Lloyd.

Lottie's head ached with tiredness and her legs felt stiff and achy from the sprint across the field from Clarendon Park. She thought of poor Mildred who'd had to get up at six and carry out her chores.

What had Harry been doing in the stables at Clarendon Park? She suspected he and his friends were up to no good. But what? And why had someone claimed he was owed three pounds? It was quite a lot of money. An amount which Mrs Moore would happily spend on a fancy new hat or handbag.

Was it possible Percy Abercromby had discovered the illicit meetings in the stables? Had he been murdered for his silence?

'Are you alright this morning, Lottie?' asked Mrs Moore. 'You're looking tired and pale.'

'I'm fine, thank you. I didn't sleep very well.'

'That's not like you! I hope you're not coming down with something.'

'I'm quite sure I'm not.'

Detective Inspector Lloyd entered the room, his pipe in his mouth.

'So what's the news?' asked Lord Buckley-Phipps. 'Have you caught him yet?'

'Not yet, my lord,' said the detective.

'But it's been five days now. He could be waiting to attack someone else!'

'Oh, good golly!' said Lady Buckley-Phipps. 'I hope not!'

'I hope not too, my lady,' said the detective.

'What about the man in the gardens?' asked the dowager.

'What man in the gardens?' asked Mrs Moore.

'Barty and I saw a man yesterday, close to the rose garden.'

'I didn't see him, Granny,' said Barty. 'I looked for him, but there was no one there.'

'But I definitely saw him,' said the dowager.

'Did he look like the man who Barty saw beneath the oak tree on the night of Percy Abercromby's murder?' asked Mrs Moore.

'I don't know,' said the dowager. 'Because I didn't see that man. But I saw the man yesterday.'

'Both were wearing dark clothing,' said the detective.

'Not a very detailed description, is it?' said Lord Buckley-Phipps. 'Have you got anything else to go on?'

'I can only use the information supplied by the eyewitnesses, my lord,' said the detective. 'But having reviewed it, I can confidently say it's likely to be the same man.'

'So he is waiting to murder someone else?' said Lady Buckley-Phipps.

'We don't know this man is the murderer, my lady,' said the detective.

'So who is he?'

'We're trying to find out.'

'You need to try harder,' said Lord Buckley-Phipps. 'My family are living in fear.'

'This is proving to be a difficult investigation,' said the detective.

'Has Lottie told you about the man she saw on the bicycle?' Mrs Moore asked the detective.

'No. Who did you see, Miss Sprigg?'

'I didn't mention it because I can't be sure,' said Lottie. 'And I'm still not sure.'

'Please tell me all the same.'

Lottie explained about the cyclist she'd seen late in the evening on the night of Percy's murder and the similarity he bore to Mr Harcourt's delivery boy, Tom Granger. 'I can't be completely sure it was him I saw that night,' she added. 'But the squeak on the bicycle sounded the same.'

The detective made a note. 'A conversation with Tom Granger should settle that one way or the other. Thank you Miss Sprigg, that's very useful.'

'I don't see why a greengrocer delivery boy would murder Percy Abercromby,' said the dowager.

'Apparently, Percy Abercromby had annoyed Mr Harcourt the greengrocer,' said Lottie. And she related the tale of the mouldy grapes and Harcourt being dropped as a supplier to Clarendon Park.

'Now that shines a more interesting light on it!' said Lord Buckley-Phipps. 'Could Harcourt have sent his boy in to murder Percy Abercromby under our roof? The cheek of it!'

'Allow me to investigate this further, my lord,' said the detective. 'This information is new to my ears.'

'It sounds like young Miss Sprigg has gathered more information than you, detective,' said Lord Buckley-Phipps. He folded his arms and glared at him.

'This is a complex investigation, my lord, with a lot to consider. Please be assured that my men and I are doing all we can to find the culprit.'

An uncomfortable silence followed.

'Well thank you, Detective,' said Lord Buckley-Phipps. 'That was most, er... helpful.'

Chapter Thirty-Three

AFTER THE MEETING with the detective, Lottie and Mrs Moore went for a walk with Rosie in the gardens. There was a breeze today and big white fluffy clouds reflected in the lake.

'Are you sure you're up for this, Lottie? I'm worried you're sickening for something.'

'I'm fine.'

'And why are you wearing such nice shoes? You usually wear your walking shoes when out with Rosie.'

Lottie thought of the shoe which had been pulled off her foot by one of the Clarendon Park dogs. Had one of the men found it? Perhaps Harry? She gave a shudder as she worried whether they could somehow trace the shoe to her.

Mrs Moore stopped. 'What is it, Lottie? You look half-miserable and half-scared. And you're wearing a pair of dainty slippers for a walk. You're not yourself at all.'

Lottie sighed and told Mrs Moore about her night-time adventure to Clarendon Park.

'So that's why I'm wearing these shoes,' she added.

'Good golly,' said her employer once she'd finished. 'You shouldn't have ventured into Clarendon Park like that! What on earth would have happened if you'd been caught? Promise me you won't try such a thing again.'

'I certainly won't be doing that again. We just wanted to find out what Harry was getting up to.'

'You mentioned money. Perhaps it's gambling or betting of some sort?'

'I suppose it must be. Maybe Percy Abercromby discovered what was going on and threatened to tell someone? Barty told me he was a telltale at school.'

'I'm sure he grew out of that. But I also feel sure that if he'd discovered something like that was going on in the stable block, then he would have done something about it. So I suppose that gives someone a motive to silence him. Harry the footman is the obvious person, isn't he? He would have known about the ornamental letter opener in the study, and he was close by when the murder took place. Golly, Lottie. You're going to have to tell Detective Inspector Lloyd about this.'

'I can't. Because the only reason I know Harry is up to something in the stables at Clarendon Park is because Mildred and I committed trespass to find out.'

'I don't think a bit of trespass matters when we're talking about murder.'

'I'd like to think about it some more before I mention it to the detective. And besides, he has Tom Granger to consider at the moment.'

'Yes, he's got the greengrocer and his delivery boy to be getting on with. Goodness, it's all quite complicated, isn't it?'

They completed a circuit of the lake and strolled towards the kitchen gardens. Rosie lagged behind them, she also seemed tired from the night-time adventure.

'I passed the orphanage when I was on the bus the other day,' said Lottie. 'And it's made me think I'd like to visit.'

'That's a nice idea, Lottie. Although you need to be careful about such things.'

'Why do you say that?'

'When we have fond memories of a place, it's not always a good idea to go back. There's a risk that it's not how you remember it. Perhaps it's changed or perhaps you've only remembered the good parts and forgotten about the bad parts. In my experience, you can never recreate a happy memory, Lottie. I think it's often best to leave it as it is. A memory.'

Lottie gave this some thought. 'I can understand that,' she said. 'It's a little over five years since I left the orphanage, so I hope it hasn't changed too much.'

'But it will have changed. And perhaps you won't mind that. But if the thought bothers you at all, then I wouldn't go back.'

'Well, I'd at least like to see Miss Beaufort and thank her for teaching me French so well. It helped us during our travels.'

'It certainly did. And she'd be delighted to see you again, I'm sure.'

Lottie wanted to add that she planned to ask Miss Beaufort about her parents. But she chose not to mention that to Mrs Moore. She worried her employer would tell her it was a bad idea.

'What's that?' said Mrs Moore. She stopped.

'What?'

'I heard a twig crack. As if someone stepped on it.' She looked around. 'It must have come from behind that tree!'

'Are you sure you're not hearing things, Mrs Moore?'

'Quite sure!' Lottie watched her employer march over to a horse chestnut tree. Its trunk was easily wide enough to conceal someone.

Lottie waited for Mrs Moore to walk around the tree and return to admit she'd been mistaken. But to Lottie's horror, a man dashed out from behind the tree and sprinted away from them towards a patch of woodland, clinging on to his hat as he went.

'Stop!' cried Mrs Moore. 'Someone stop that man!'

But there was no one else around to hear and Lottie had no hope of chasing after him, he was too fast. In no time at all, he reached the woods and disappeared between the trees.

Mrs Moore stared at Lottie, open-mouthed. 'Did you see him, Lottie? What was he doing? Was he planning to ambush us?'

Chapter Thirty-Four

'WHAT DID HE LOOK LIKE?' asked Lord Buckley-Phipps.

'He was wearing dark clothing,' said Mrs Moore.

'That description again. Anything else?'

'And a hat. He sprinted away from us, he was gone in a matter of seconds. I only wish I'd got a better look at him.'

Lord Buckley-Phipps sighed. 'I'll telephone Detective Inspector Lloyd. And I'll tell him that we need every policeman in Shropshire searching our grounds! This man is a pest. What's he doing creeping around the gardens and frightening the ladies? We should all arm ourselves with guns.'

'We can't shoot him, Ivan!' said Lady Buckley-Phipps.

'Why not? He's a menace!'

'We can't take the law into our own hands.'

'Well, the detective is doing nothing about it, is he? Hopeless. I've a good mind to telephone Scotland Yard and personally request one of their best.'

Chapter Thirty-Five

BARTY BUCKLEY-PHIPPS SAUNTERED down Hambledon Hill, hoping his stroll might coincide with Evelyn Abercromby's ride. To his delight, it wasn't long before he saw her on her horse trotting towards him. He felt even happier when she slowed to a stop.

'Hello, Barty!'

'Hello, Evelyn. How are you and your family faring?'

'As well as can be, thank you.'

'Oh good. I can't imagine what it must be like.'

'There's no need for you to imagine, Barty. Instead, just enjoy spending time with your family. You don't know how long you'll have them with you for.'

'Gosh. That's a profound statement, Evelyn. I shall take your advice.'

'And you needn't worry so much about my parents blaming you for Percy's death, Barty. They've decided someone else might be responsible.'

'Who?'

'Someone who tried to kill Percy a few weeks ago.'

'Good grief, really? What happened?'

'Well, I thought little of it at the time, I just thought it was Percy being melodramatic about things. But now I realise it was probably an attempt on his life.'

'Tell me what happened!'

'He was walking through the village when someone drove a van at him. He managed to leap out of the way just in time.'

'That's awful! Who was driving the van?'

'It was Mr Harcourt, the greengrocer. And Percy knew it was him because the name was written on the side.'

'Mr Harcourt tried to kill him?'

'Mr Harcourt claimed it was an accident and that he'd been distracted by a wasp buzzing around the steering wheel while he was driving. As he'd tried to swat it away, he'd accidentally nudged the wheel and nearly knocked into Percy on the pavement. But Percy said he was sure the grocer did it deliberately. Percy said he had murderous intent in his eyes as he drove at him.'

'Crikey. This is making sense, now.'

'Is it?'

'Just this morning, Lottie told us all about Percy trying to buy grapes from Mr Harcourt for half their price. He claimed they were mouldy.'

Evelyn rolled her eyes. 'That sounds like Percy.'

'But Mr Harcourt refused, so Percy apparently persuaded the cook at Clarendon Park to change the greengrocer supplier.'

'So that's why the supplier changed? I had no idea it had anything to do with Percy complaining about mouldy grapes.'

'Apparently, Mr Harcourt lost a lot of business and I shouldn't think he ever forgave him.'

'So Mr Harcourt, the greengrocer, could be the murderer?'

'Either him or his delivery boy who Lottie saw leaving the house late that night.'

'Gosh.'

'Does Detective Inspector Lloyd know about the van incident?'

'Yes.'

'Good. Because he also knows about the mouldy grape incident. Hopefully, it's solved! I'll tell Lottie what you've told me because she's very clever with these sorts of things. She's solved a few murders.'

'Really?'

'I don't know how she does it. It's the way her mind works, I suppose. She's got more brain cells than me in her little finger.'

Evelyn laughed. 'No one has brain cells in their finger, Barty!'

'No I suppose not.'

'You are funny.'

'Am I?' He felt his face heat up. 'I'll take that as a compliment.'

Chapter Thirty-Six

TOM GRANGER FOLDED his arms and scowled at Detective Inspector Lloyd. The pair of them were sitting in a little room in Lowton Chorley police station. The detective took a sip of tea, then puffed on his pipe.

'I don't understand why I'm here,' said Tom.

'I've already told you that all will become clear.'

'I hope so, because I've done nothing wrong. And Mr Harcourt needs me for his deliveries today.'

'I won't detain you for long.' The detective consulted his notebook. 'So we've established that you visited Fortescue Manor on the day Mr Abercromby was murdered.'

'Yes. In the morning to deliver fruit and vegetables for the dinner.'

'And you think you got there at eleven o'clock.'

'Yes.'

'And you stayed for about twenty minutes. That's quite a long time.'

'I had a glass of lemonade there and chatted to one of the maids.'

'Which one?'

'I don't know her name.' This was a lie and luckily the detective appeared to accept it.

'Where did you go after you made the delivery?'

'Back to the shop.'

'And what time did you get back?'

'I didn't look at the time when I got back, but it was probably around midday.'

'And did you return to Fortescue Manor that day?'

Tom knew what was coming. 'No.'

'Are you sure?'

'Very sure.'

'So how do you explain why someone saw you at Fortescue Manor late that evening?'

His stomach lurched. 'Who saw me there?'

'I'm not at liberty to say.'

'Well, whoever it was is mistaken. I wasn't there.'

'So where were you at that time?'

'In the pub.'

'Which one?'

'The Three Oaks.'

'Is there someone who can verify you were there?'

'Yes.' Now he would have to find his friend Jack to make sure he could cover for him.

'And you're sure you weren't at Fortescue Manor that evening?'

'Completely sure, sir.'

'The witness described you cycling away.'

He faked a laugh. 'Why would I have been there?'

'Are you saying the witness is mistaken?'

'They must have seen someone else.'

'Apparently your bicycle has a distinctive squeak.'

Tom felt his shoulders slump. He'd been meaning to oil that squeak for weeks. 'I wasn't at Fortescue Manor that evening. Jack will tell you.'

'I look forward to it. How well did you know Mr Abercromby?'

'I didn't know him at all.'

'He visited Harcourt's greengrocers.'

Tom shrugged. 'Doesn't mean I knew him.'

'Were you aware Mr Abercromby complained about the grocer's shop?'

'Yes, I think Mr Harcourt said something about that.'

'As a result of Mr Abercromby's complaint, Mr Harcourt lost the agreement to supply Clarendon Park. He must have been upset about that.'

How did the detective know all this? Tom pulled at his earlobe and chose his words carefully. 'You'd have to ask Mr Harcourt about that, sir.'

Mr Harcourt was going to have to tell the detective a few lies. Trade had been difficult in recent months and losing Clarendon Park as a customer had knocked a lot off the greengrocer's income.

Percy Abercromby hadn't cared about that. All he'd wanted were some cheap grapes. It would have been better if Mr Harcourt had given into Percy, but Tom could understand why he hadn't. Why should ordinary people have to be subservient to the rich and powerful? He admired Mr Harcourt for having stood his ground.

But now Mr Harcourt had to make money in other ways, and the work wasn't always legal. Tom blamed Percy Abercromby for the plight his employer was in. He would never forget the smile on Mr Harcourt's face when he'd heard the young man was dead.

'So you can't tell me anything more about Percy Abercromby's complaint?' asked the detective.

'No. I didn't take too much interest in it. I just work in the shop and do the deliveries.'

Chapter Thirty-Seven

THE FOLLOWING DAY, Lottie and Rosie took the bus into Oswestry. As they trundled through the countryside, Lottie couldn't stop thinking about the man who'd been lurking behind the horse chestnut tree.

Had he been following Lottie and Mrs Moore? Or had he been waiting there for someone else? Either way, Lottie found it unsettling. It was the third time he'd been seen in the gardens, and yet he disappeared whenever someone wished to challenge him.

Lord Buckley-Phipps had arranged for the police to search the grounds, but Lottie felt sure the man would be good at hiding from them.

She and Rosie got off the bus outside the red brick orphanage. As she walked through the gate and up the path, the building seemed smaller than she'd remembered.

The lady who answered the door gasped with astonishment. 'It's not, is it? Is it really you, Lottie Sprigg?'

'Yes, it is. Hello Sally.'

Sally was a plump, fair-haired lady who had looked after the orphanage children for many years.

'You must come in and join us for a cup of tea!' Rosie wagged her tail. 'And your friend too!' said Sally, smiling at the dog.

'Is Miss Beaufort here today?' Lottie asked, as she followed Sally to the sitting room. She'd never been allowed into the sitting room as a child, but she had often chatted to the staff at its doorway.

'Yes, she is,' said Sally. 'I'll fetch her. I know she'd be delighted to see you.'

She showed Lottie and Rosie into the comfortable sitting room with shabby chairs and plump cushions. Tall windows overlooked the garden where children were playing.

Lottie sat down in a tweed covered armchair. 'I grew up in this place,' she said to Rosie, who rested by her feet. She didn't expect the corgi to understand what she was saying.

Miss Beaufort swept into the room, arms outstretched for an embrace. Lottie stood up and hugged her former schoolmistress.

'How lovely it is to see you again, Lottie!' she said once she'd disentangled herself. She was just as Lottie had remembered her with her French accent, wavy grey hair and smile lines at her eyes. She perched on the chair next to her. 'I heard from one of the maids at Fortescue Manor that you're now employed as a travelling companion to Lady Buckley-Phipps' sister! And what a lovely dog you have!'

'She's called Rosie,' said Lottie. 'We adopted her in Venice.'

'She's a Venetian dog? She must find Shropshire very different. There's only one canal here, and it's not quite the same as Venice, is it?'

'No, but she enjoys the countryside walks. I'd like to say thank you, Miss Beaufort, for teaching me French so well. It really helped us on our travels.'

'I'm so pleased it was helpful! You were a good student, Lottie.'

Over tea, Sally and Miss Beaufort asked Lottie about her travels. 'I can't imagine seeing all those places,' said Sally. 'How fascinating it must have been.'

'And well-deserved,' said Miss Beaufort. 'You were always destined for better things.'

'I don't know about that.'

'You were! I remember you reading the books from the library. We didn't have many books here back then, but you read each of them many times over. It was good of Mrs Moore to take you under her wing. It's no more than you deserve.'

'Being away from home made me think about a few things. I reflected on my childhood and feel pleased it was so happy.'

'That's wonderful to hear, Lottie. Not everyone who's grown up in an orphanage can say that.'

'And I also wondered if I would ever be able to find out who my parents were. I was left as a baby on the doorstep here, wasn't I?'

The smile faded from Miss Beaufort's face. 'Yes, you were. We found you wrapped in a blanket in a box. You'd been well looked after, you were clean and well-fed. I should think your mother was reluctant to leave you with us because she'd clearly looked after you.'

'Was there any clue who she could have been?'

'Not to my knowledge. If you want to talk about it some more, then we'll have to ask Miss Spencer.'

Lottie wasn't keen on Miss Spencer. She was the lady who managed the orphanage. She was austere and strict and, fortunately, had little to do with the children.

'I'll go and fetch her,' said Sally. She left the room before Lottie could protest.

'It's a rule Miss Spencer has,' said Miss Beaufort. 'If

anyone wants to know more about their circumstances, then she must be consulted. Sally and I... well, we just work here.' She gave Lottie a smile which seemed like an attempt to reassure.

Moments later, Miss Spencer stepped into the room. She had a gaunt, lined face and wore a dark, old-fashioned dress. Lottie got to her feet and Rosie remained by her side.

'Miss Sprigg,' she said. 'I hear you've done well for yourself.'

'Hello Miss Spencer. Thank you.'

'Sally tells me you would like to know more about your mother.'

'If possible.'

'I'm sure you know the most common reasons why a mother may be unable to look after her child. Perhaps you were born out of wedlock. Or maybe your family was too poor to look after you. Your mother may even have kept you a secret from everyone she knew. By leaving you on our doorstep, she hoped we could give you a better upbringing than she could.'

'When I was left in the box, were there any clues about who she could have been?'

'None.' Her response was curt. Then she gave a thin smile. 'I'm sorry, Miss Sprigg, but that's often the way. No clue would have been left because your mother wouldn't have wanted to be found. You would have been her disgrace, I'm afraid.'

Chapter Thirty-Eight

'WHERE'VE YOU BEEN?' said Mr Harcourt when Tom returned to the greengrocer's shop. 'I've had Mrs Cartwright on the telephone asking about her delivery.'

'I'll do it now. I had to speak to Detective Inspector Lloyd.'

Mr Harcourt fixed him with his steely eyes. 'What did he want?'

'Someone says they saw me at Fortescue Manor the other evening.'

'Someone saw you?'

'I've already spoken to Jack, and he's going to give me an alibi for that evening.'

'He's going to lie for you?'

Tom nodded. 'He owes me a favour.'

'You asked Jack for an alibi, so he knows you were up to something. Did you tell him where you were?'

'I told him I was out poaching and that I need him to tell the police I was with him in the pub.'

Mr Harcourt pulled a grimace. 'Let's hope he doesn't ask

you any more questions about it. It's a shame you were seen. Do you know who saw you?'

'Detective wouldn't tell me.'

'Because I had some young woman from Fortescue Manor asking me questions the other day. She used to work there as a maid and she works for Lady Buckley-Phipps' sister now. What's her name...' He drummed his thick fingers on the counter as he thought. 'Lottie Sprigg. Have you met her?'

'I think I remember seeing her at the house when she worked as a maid.'

'She asked me a really strange question. She asked me if we did evening deliveries. I thought it was odd at the time, but now it makes sense. She was the one who must have seen you that evening.'

Tom clenched his teeth. 'And she's told the detective about me!'

'So now they know you were at the house when Percy Abercromby was murdered. This doesn't look good for us, Tom.'

'I know.'

'And there's something funny about Lottie Sprigg,' said Mr Harcourt. 'She asked me about Percy Abercromby. She'd heard the story about the grapes.'

'From who?'

'I don't know. People talk about anything in this village. Nothing stays secret, does it?'

'No.'

'We can only hope the detective believes Jack as your alibi. But it's not good when you've got to ask someone to lie for you. It means they've got information they can use against you if need be.' He removed his cap and ran his hand over his smooth head. 'And Lottie Sprigg knows we were angry at Percy Abercromby and she knows you were at the house on the night he was murdered. She needs to mind her own business.'

'I'll ask Tilly to keep an eye on her.'

The greengrocer replaced his cap. 'That would be helpful. Get her to report back to you.'

'I will. Tilly does everything I say.'

Chapter Thirty-Nine

LOTTIE SAW HARRY in the saloon when she returned to Fortescue Manor.

Instead of greeting her, the footman paused and looked her up and down. Lottie was in no mood for his hostility. Miss Spencer's harsh words rung in her ears and she had cried a little on the bus on the way back. Mrs Moore had been right. It was often a mistake returning to places from the past.

Harry looked at Rosie and narrowed his eyes. 'Your dog,' he said. 'Was she out the other night?'

'I don't think so. What are you referring to?'

He gave a sniff. 'Some friends of mine were troubled by a dog the other night. And the description sounded like a corgi.'

'Rosie wouldn't trouble anyone.'

'You can't trust any dog completely.'

'She wasn't out the other night. She's with me all the time.' She gave him a defiant stare, but her heart pounded in her chest.

'They found a woman's shoe,' he said.

'Why are you telling me this?'

'Just wondered if you knew anyone who was missing one.'

'Lottie!' She had never been more relieved to hear Barty's voice. He strode over to them. 'Hello Harry.'

'Hello, sir.' Harry gave a nod and went on his way. Barty pulled a puzzled expression. 'What was he talking to you about, Lottie?'

'One of his friends thought he saw Rosie somewhere, but I told him it wasn't her and...' The rest of Lottie's sentence was swallowed by a sob.

'Oh Lottie, what's the matter?' Barty pulled a large, fresh handkerchief from his pocket and put his arm across her shoulders. 'Come and sit down. What's upset you?'

It took Lottie a minute or two to recover.

'You don't have to tell me what's upset you if you don't want to. I know some ladies can be a little embarrassed about sharing some things with a gentleman.'

Lottie looked up at him. 'It's quite alright. I went to the orphanage and perhaps I shouldn't have.'

'Oh.'

'I wanted to ask about my mother.' Her throat tightened, and she didn't want to say anything more for fear of bursting into tears again.

'Oh. I see now why it's upset you,' said Barty. 'I can understand why you want to know about her. Finding the answers to such things can be difficult. But if it helps, I want you to know you have a family here, Lottie. Auntie adores you. And I told you in Vienna that I think of you as a sister these days. Think of Fortescue Manor as your home now. As heir to this place, I insist on it.'

Lottie gave another sob.

'Oh dear,' said Barty. 'Perhaps my words aren't helping.'

'No they are, Barty.' She smiled at him. 'Please believe it, they're helping a lot.'

Chapter Forty

TOM GRANGER STEERED his bicycle around the side of Fortescue Manor and turned again into the servants' courtyard. Edward the footman had to leap out of his path.

'Crikey!' he said. 'You nearly knocked me over! Usually I hear your bicycle before I see it. Have you fixed that squeak?'

'Certainly have,' said Tom. He dismounted, leant his bicycle against the wall, pulled a bag out of his basket and skipped down the steps which led to the kitchen.

The chubby, freckle-faced maid, Mildred, was in there with the housekeeper.

'Hello Tom,' said Mrs Hudson. 'Are we expecting a delivery from you?'

'I got a message that you needed potatoes.'

'Potatoes? I think we're alright for potatoes.'

'Well, I had a message saying you needed some urgently. Maybe Tilly would know about it?'

The housekeeper turned to Mildred. 'Perhaps you can fetch her and see what this is about.'

'I'll wait in the courtyard,' he said.

He went back outside and asked Edward for a cigarette. 'Don't you have to get back to work?' he said.

'I've got another five minutes yet.'

'I need a word with Tilly.' He gave a wink to make Edward understand.

'Oh, I see.' Edward slunk away just as Tilly climbed the steps from the kitchen.

'What's this about potatoes?' she asked.

'Keep your voice down.'

'What?' she whispered.

'Lottie Sprigg has been talking to the police about me.'

'Has she?'

'She saw me here that night.'

'Oh no!'

'If she asks you about it, I was never here.'

'Alright. I know to keep it secret.'

'Good. And keep an eye on her for me.'

'How do you mean?'

'Just let me know what she's up to.' He puffed out a cloud of smoke.

'Not much, I don't think. She takes her dogs out for walks and she's gone down to the village a few times.'

'She's talking to people.'

'That's normal, isn't it?'

'Depends on what she's talking about.'

'She writes things in notebooks.'

'Does she? Perhaps you can get hold of them for me.'

'Steal them?'

'You know what I mean. What have you got for me today?'

She took something out of her apron pocket and he held out his hand for it.

'A snuff box? Is that it?'

'It's silver.'

161

'I know it's silver. But I can't go back with a snuff box and nothing else!'

'It's been a difficult few days. The detective's been in the house and there've been policemen here too. It's not been easy.'

'I'm going to get into trouble over this. Just one snuff box? I know what they've got in that house, you can do better than this.'

'How do you know what they've got?'

He lowered his voice. 'Because I've crept in and had a look round, haven't I?' Tom felt proud of his stealthy skills. He'd sneaked up the service stairs and visited rooms when the house was quiet. He'd been through drawers and cupboards and taken little valuable things no one would miss. He'd almost been caught a few times, but he was good at hiding behind curtains and furniture.

He didn't have as many opportunities as Tilly though, and that's why he'd recruited her. Unfortunately she wasn't doing as well as he'd hoped she would.

'I want to stop taking things.' She pushed her lower lip out.

'You can't.'

'What do you mean, I can't? I can if I like. I don't want to do it anymore. I want to stop while no one's noticed. I'm worried I'm going to take something and someone's going to realise it was me. Then I'd be for it!'

'You can't stop, Tilly. I've got orders to collect more from you.'

'From who?'

'You know I can't say. But you're being paid for this, so you need to do what we agreed. You still haven't got me the key to the silver vault. How long is it since I asked for that? Two weeks?'

'I've looked for it in Mr Duxbury's office, but I couldn't find it anywhere. He's got it well hidden somewhere.'

'Keep on looking.'

'It's not easy! I'm not allowed in the butler's rooms and if anyone sees me near there, then they'll be suspicious. Mildred has already seen me there.'

'What did she say?'

'She was surprised, and I told her I'd dared myself to go there. She believed me, but also thought it was a strange thing to do.'

'You need to be careful, Tilly, you don't want to get caught.'

'No I don't. And that's why I want to stop!'

He sighed. Tilly had been paid too well. Presumably she'd saved what she'd been given, and no longer felt the need for anything more.

'I don't want you to stop until you find the key to the silver vault. Once you've found it, you can stop.'

'It's difficult.'

'You're a maid. You can go everywhere in the house. Can't you pretend you need to go in there to do some dusting?'

'Mr Duxbury prefers to do that himself.'

'If you don't get the key for me, Tilly, there'll be trouble.'

'What sort of trouble?'

'I'll tell people you're a thief.'

'No, you can't do that! I'll lose my job!'

'Then you need to find the key.'

'If you tell people I'm a thief, then I shall say the same about you!'

'They won't believe you. Harcourt will vouch for me. Who's going to defend you? No one.'

Tilly's face crumpled. 'I don't understand why you're being so nasty! I used to think you were nice. That's why I agreed to it. But ever since I started thieving for you, you've turned into a nasty person!'

She was right. She'd realised now he'd only befriended her because he knew he could persuade her to steal.

'Do you know what I think?' she said.

'What?'

'I think you could be the murderer.'

'What?'

'You were in the house that evening. I think Percy Abercromby saw you take something and so you murdered him.'

'I'm not a murderer!'

'I think you are because I've realised how nasty you are!'

He lowered his voice. 'I'm not the murderer, Tilly, because I know who the murderer is.'

Her eyes grew wide. 'You do?'

'I saw them.'

'When?'

'That night.'

'Who is it?'

'I can't say. It's too dangerous. We were both in places we weren't supposed to be. I'd be in trouble. Big trouble. But I'll tell you if you get that key for me.'

'You will?'

'I promise.'

Chapter Forty-One

LOTTIE AND ROSIE sat with Mrs Moore and the dowager in the sitting room before dinner. She'd told her employer about her visit to the orphanage, and Mrs Moore had responded that Miss Spencer seemed a cold-hearted woman.

Lottie had felt comforted by her response. Perhaps it was best that she put thoughts of her mother out of her mind.

'Do we know if the police have caught that man yet?' asked the dowager.

'Not that I've heard,' said Mrs Moore.

'I wonder what's taking them so long.' The dowager sighed. 'I just hope no one else is murdered.'

'So do I!' said Mrs Moore.

Barty entered the room. 'Lottie! Just the person I need to see. There's something I meant to tell you earlier, but... well, it wasn't the right time. I spoke to Evelyn Abercromby the other day.'

'You saw Evelyn Abercromby?' asked Mrs Moore.

'Yes, she was riding her horse.'

'And how is she?'

'She's alright, under the circumstances.' He pulled at his collar. 'I've bumped into her a few times.'

'Really?' said the dowager.

'My walks and her rides seem to coincide.'

'Well, that's a happy coincidence,' said Mrs Moore.

Barty flushed red. 'Anyway,' he said. 'She told me an interesting tale about Mr Harcourt, the greengrocer and Percy Abercromby.'

Lottie listened intently as Barty told them about a supposed attempt Mr Harcourt had made to hit Percy Abercromby with his van.

'How very interesting,' said Mrs Moore.

'It is, isn't it? Detective Inspector Lloyd has all the information, so hopefully he'll be making an arrest soon.'

'That would be nice,' said the dowager. 'But if Harcourt and his boy are the murderers, how do you explain the man in the grounds?'

'I don't know, Granny.'

'And I've just had another thought,' said Lottie. 'We know the murderer fled the library and knocked her ladyship over before running out of the door. If Tom was the murderer, why would he return to the house after that?'

'To demonstrate he wasn't the murderer?' said Barty. You would expect the murderer to flee and get away from the house as far as possible. So anyone who remained in the house after the murder could be deemed innocent. Perhaps he wanted to be seen in the house? Then no one could suspect him.'

'But did anyone else see him in the house? I heard him speak to someone else. In fact, I think he raised his voice at them.'

'We need to find that person,' said the dowager.

'And why haven't they come forward sooner?' said Mrs Moore.

'They must be hiding something,' said Lottie. 'I wonder who it is?'

'Perhaps it's Harry,' said Mrs Moore. 'I saw the detective earlier and mentioned Harry's late night antics to him.'

'Late night antics?' said Barty. 'What's he been doing?'

'I heard he was discussing money late in the night in the stables at Clarendon Park. I suspect it was something to do with betting or gambling.'

Lottie felt relieved that Mrs Moore didn't mention her trespassing.

'Goodness,' said Barty, wiping his brow. 'Isn't it astonishing what people get up to?'

Chapter Forty-Two

MILDRED FOUND Lottie at breakfast the following morning. 'We need your help!' she said. 'The key to the silver vault is missing.'

The silver vault was a secure room by the butler's office. The family's priceless silver collection was kept there.

'Why do you think Lottie can find it?' said Mrs Moore.

'Because Lottie's good at this sort of thing.'

'But Lottie's eating her breakfast.'

'I've pretty much finished,' said Lottie, cramming the last bit of toast into her mouth. She wiped her hands on her serviette and rested it next to her plate on the table. Then she and Rosie followed Mildred out of the room and down the service staircase.

'I think Tilly could be involved,' whispered Mildred as they went. 'But I don't know whether to confront her!'

'If she is, then perhaps she can be persuaded to admit it?' said Lottie.

'How do we do that?'

'I don't know yet.'

In the servants' hall, the discussion was lively.

'The last time I saw it was yesterday,' said Mr Duxbury. 'It was on the little hook inside my wardrobe.'

'It has to be one of the servants,' said Mrs Hudson.

Lottie spotted Tilly in the corner of the room, biting her lip.

'Or perhaps someone didn't take it,' continued the house-keeper. 'Perhaps you've absent-mindedly put it down some-where, Mr Duxbury?'

'I never absent-mindedly put anything down anywhere!'

'Right. Come on everyone, look for the key.'

'All the servants' bedrooms must be searched!' said the butler. 'You and I will do that Mrs Hudson, and every servant must remain in this room while we do it.'

'We have to stay here?' said Harry.

'That's what Mr Duxbury says,' said Edward.

Tilly said nothing.

The housekeeper and butler left the room. Mildred gave Lottie a questioning glance.

'Ask her about it,' whispered Lottie in reply.

Mildred cleared her throat. 'Don't think badly of me for asking you this Tilly,' she said. 'But have you got the key?'

'Me? No! Why would I have the key?'

'You're accusing Tilly?' said Harry.

'Yes,' said Mildred, her voice shaking a little. 'Because I saw Tilly coming out of Mr Duxbury's rooms the other day. You told me you did it as a dare, didn't you Tilly? But I think you were looking for the key.'

'No! I would never do it!'

'That's a serious accusation, Mildred,' said Harry. 'You should be careful what you accuse people of.'

Mildred gulped, then continued. 'There was the hair comb that time, as well.'

'I forgot to return it! I told you that!'

'But I don't just think it was the hair comb, was it, Tilly? I think you've taken other things too.'

'Are you calling me a thief?'

'Am I right?'

'And to think I thought you were a friend, Mildred!'

'I am. And I'm disappointed that a friend of mine has become a thief. You've got the key haven't you?'

Tilly's lower lip wobbled in reply.

'Please just hand back the key,' said Mildred. 'Then this can all be sorted out without any trouble.'

'You don't understand!'

'I'm sure I will if you explain.'

'Tilly does have the key?' said Harry, his mouth hanging open. 'I'll go and fetch Mr Duxbury and Mrs Hudson.'

A little while later, everyone sat around the table in the servants' hall. Tilly was sobbing into her handkerchief and the key lay in the middle of the table.

'Someone made me do it!' said Tilly.

'Who?' asked the housekeeper.

'I can't say.'

'Well if you're not going to say, then you're the one who's going to be in trouble.'

'They told me they saw the murderer.'

'What?' said Mr Duxbury.

'Apparently he saw the murderer, and he said he'd tell me who the murderer was when I got him the key.'

'If he saw the murderer, then why hasn't he told the police?' said Mr Duxbury.

'Because he's too scared. He might get into trouble.'

'Well whoever he is, he's already in a lot of trouble. Why on earth did he ask you to take the key to the silver vault? Did he plan to steal something from there?'

'I suppose so.'

'I think it's quite obvious that's what he planned to do,' said the housekeeper.

'Who is this man?' asked Mr Duxbury.

'I really can't say! I'll be in so much trouble!'

'You're already in trouble, young miss!'

'Can I suggest something?' said Lottie. All the faces turned to her. 'Why don't we let Tilly give him the key?'

'Outrageous!' said Mr Duxbury.

'Not if he knows who the murderer is.'

'But does he really know?' said Mrs Hudson. 'Or is he just saying it to get the key?'

'We can't be sure,' said Lottie. 'But I think it's worth a try. And then perhaps you could get the lock changed on the door to the silver vault.'

'That's a bit of trouble to go to,' grumbled the butler.

'It's not really though, is it Mr Duxbury?' said the house-keeper. 'If this person can tell Tilly who the murderer is, then the case is solved.'

'Very well,' said the butler. 'But this doesn't mean you're out of trouble, Tilly. Give him the key and tell us what he tells you. In the meantime, I'll get the lock changed. But don't let onto him about any of this! Will you tell us who this man is?'

Tilly shook her head. 'I'll get him into trouble.'

'Well if he really knows who the murderer is then he'll have to speak to the detective about it,' said Mrs Hudson. 'We'll find out who it is soon enough. But for the time being, Tilly, you play along with his game.'

Chapter Forty-Three

LATER THAT DAY, Harry was summoned to the music room.

'We meet again Harry Lewis,' said Detective Inspector Lloyd, puffing on his pipe.

Harry sat down opposite him. 'What's this about, sir?'

'I've had a report that you were seen in the grounds of Clarendon Park three nights ago. Can you explain what you were doing on the Abercromby family estate?'

Harry swallowed. That girl Lottie Sprigg had told the police about him! He felt sure she'd followed him there that night. He'd seen her dog and found her shoe.

'No, there must be some mistake. Who supposedly saw me?'

'I'm not at liberty to say. But there is a report of someone matching your description visiting the stables and discussing money.'

Harry laughed. 'Discussing money? Is that a crime?'

'If it's connected to illegal betting, it is.'

'What makes you think I'm involved in something like

that? And besides, it wasn't me. I've got no reason to visit Clarendon.'

'The person who saw you was quite convinced it was you.'

'Even so, they must be mistaken. Presumably it was dark? It's easy to be mistaken in the dark.'

'When did you last visit Clarendon Park?'

'Probably a few years ago.'

'Do you know anyone who lives on the estate?'

He realised there was no use in completely lying. 'I know Smithy.'

'Smithy?'

'Stephen Smith. He's a stableboy there.'

'So, were you visiting him on the night you were seen in the grounds?'

'No! I wasn't there.'

'And what will Smithy say when I ask him about it?'

'I don't know!' Harry could only hope he could get to Smithy before the detective did.

'You don't know? If you weren't there, then surely he'll deny it, too?'

'Of course he would.'

The detective put his pipe in his mouth and flipped through his notebook. 'I find you a difficult man to pin down, Harry. It looks like you've been up to something you can't properly explain again. On the night of Percy Abercromby's murder, you claimed to be checking the dining room even though the butler had already done it. So you were either in the dining room for another reason, or you were in the library murdering Percy Abercromby!'

'I wasn't!'

'And now we have a report of a night-time excursion to Clarendon Park. I really don't see why someone would say you were there if you weren't.'

'Perhaps someone's got it in for me?'

'Who?'

'I don't know.'

The detective leant forward. 'You're hiding something, Harry, I know it. Did you have a reason to murder Percy Abercromby?'

'No.' The image flashed into his mind again. Percy laughing arm-in-arm with Daisy as they strolled along Lowton Chorley high street together. Harry had seen them from the other side of the street. His heart raced as he recalled how he'd confronted them. Daisy had been apologetic and ashamed. But Percy had just given him a smug smile.

'I think Daisy has chosen someone else now.' Those had been his words!

Harry's jaw clenched.

'As the person who found Mr Abercromby, you were well placed to attack him, weren't you?' asked the detective.

'I may have been. But I raised the alarm! If I was the murderer, I wouldn't have raised the alarm, would I? I would have run away and left someone else to find him.'

'Perhaps you raised the alarm so no one would suspect you?'

'I don't think I'm clever enough to think of that, Detective.'

'No? I think you're cleverer than you appear to be, Harry Lewis.'

Chapter Forty-Four

LOTTIE FELT restless the next day, wondering when Tilly would be told who the murderer was in return for the key to the silver vault. She took Rosie for a stroll in the gardens and tried to distract her mind from thinking about the case. It had consumed her thoughts for over a week and, although there were some suspects, she felt frustrated there was no firm evidence yet.

She glanced over her shoulder as she walked, wondering if the dark suited man would make an appearance again. For this reason, she walked close to the house so she could run back to it quickly if something alarmed her. It was a shame she couldn't enjoy the gardens as much as she had done in the past.

Rosie was unbothered, though. She sniffed the lavender and had a skip around in the rose garden. The dowager was doing a good job of maintaining it, the roses looked like they would bloom long into late summer.

'Lottie!' Mildred was sprinting across the lawn to her. 'Lottie!'

'What is it?' she ran over to her, alarmed by the urgency in her voice.

When they met, Mildred was so puffed out she could barely speak. 'You won't believe it,' she panted. 'But Tom Granger's dead!'

'Dead?'

'He came off his bicycle at the bottom of Hambledon Hill!' Her eyes filled with tears. 'Isn't it awful?'

Chapter Forty-Five

'HERE'S what we know so far,' said Detective Inspector Lloyd. Everyone was gathered in the drawing room, the servants and the family members.

'Tom Granger, Harcourt the greengrocer's delivery boy, delivered some fruit and vegetables to the house at eleven o'clock this morning. He left his bicycle in the servants' court-yard and was in the house for about five minutes while he had a glass of lemonade and chatted to the servants. Who here spoke to him?'

Tilly, Mildred and Edward raised their hands.

'Tom Granger then made his way back to Lowton Chorley,' said the detective. 'A young lady out riding spotted him lying by a gate at the bottom of Hambledon Hill.'

'A young lady out riding?' said Barty. 'It wasn't Evelyn Abercromby, was it?'

'As a matter of fact, it was,' said the detective. 'She jumped down from her horse to see if she could help the young man, but sadly she couldn't. His bicycle was badly damaged. The gate is on a sharp bend at the bottom of the hill, I'm sure many of you are familiar with it. It seems the young man was unable to safely negotiate the bend.'

Lottie heard a sob. She turned to see Mildred comforting Tilly.

'A quick examination of the bicycle has revealed an obvious fault,' said the detective. 'The brake cables had been cut.'

Gasps sounded throughout the room.

'We don't know when the cables were cut,' said the detective. 'But Tom Granger safely bicycled here this morning without incident. My assumption is that the cables were cut while his bicycle rested in the servants' courtyard.'

'That man!' said Lord Buckley-Phipps.

'Which man, my lord?'

'The man who's been roaming the gardens for the last week. Who else? He waited for his opportunity and he got it!'

'You think he could be responsible?'

'He has to be! And if you'd caught him, then another young man needn't have lost his life!'

'We've been doing all we can, my lord.'

'It's not enough! I've said it before, but now I'm definitely going to act. I'm going to telephone Scotland Yard and get them to send their very best detective here. It's a nonsense! Who's he going to attack next?'

'No one I hope!' said Lady Buckley-Phipps. 'Oh, it's awful!'

'Dreadful,' said the dowager. 'His death could have been avoided if the murderer had been caught sooner.'

'I'd like to say something,' said a small voice. Everyone turned and Lottie realised it was Tilly who had spoken. She rubbed her nose with a handkerchief and continued.

'I fell in love with Tom Granger,' she said. 'I thought it was love at the time. I realise now maybe it wasn't. But he asked me to steal for him.'

'Steal?' said Lady Buckley-Phipps.

'I'm very sorry, my lady,' said Tilly. 'I'm very ashamed of myself. I wish I'd never got caught up with him. I agreed to do it for money. And then he asked me to steal the key to the silver vault for him.'

'*What*?' said Lord Buckley-Phipps.

'We found out about it, my lord,' added Mr Duxbury. 'The young man had told Tilly that he'd seen the murderer and would tell her who it was when she got him the key.' He turned to Tilly. 'Did you give him the key, Tilly?'

She gave a sniff. 'Yes, I did.'

'The plan, my lord, was for Tilly to give Tom the key and we would change the lock on the silver vault so he couldn't access it.'

'I see. So did Tom tell her who the murderer is?'

'Tilly?' said Mr Duxbury.

Lottie held her breath, straining to hear Tilly's quiet voice. She sniffed. 'No.'

'Did you ask him?'

'Yes. And he looked for a moment like he was going to tell me, but then he said he couldn't.'

'So it was a lie all along!' said Mrs Hudson.

'Perhaps he was the murderer himself?' said Mrs Moore. 'After all, he was here at the house on the night Percy Abercromby died.'

'He came here to see me that night,' said Tilly. 'I had some things to give him which I'd taken. But it wasn't enough, and he was angry with me.'

Lottie realised now this was the raised voice she'd heard.

'So he wasn't the murderer, and he didn't see the murderer,' said Mrs Hudson. 'What a waste of time.'

'It's another tragic waste of life,' said Lottie. 'But I think he did see the murderer.'

'What makes you say that?'

'It could be the reason he was murdered.'

'POOR EVELYN!' said Barty once the detective and servants had left the drawing room. 'It must have been awful for her discovering Tom Granger at the bottom of the hill. And just think, if she'd been there moments earlier, then he'd have hurtled right into her and her horse! What a frightening thought!'

'Very frightening,' said Lord Buckley-Phipps. 'The Abercrombys could have lost another child.'

'It just shows how selfish this murderer is!' said Barty. 'They didn't care about Tom and neither did they care that the accident could have harmed other people too. They need to be stopped!'

'I'll make my telephone call to Scotland Yard now,' said Lord Buckley-Phipps, getting to his feet. 'That man has to be caught.'

'But who is he?' said Lady Buckley-Phipps.

'No one knows, do they, dear? That's why we need an experienced detective from the Yard.'

He left the room and Mrs Moore gave a sigh. 'So terribly sad,' she said. 'That young man clearly knew something.'

'He was a common thief!' said Lady Buckley-Phipps. 'And he persuaded one of our maids to steal from us!'

'But he didn't deserve to die, Lucinda. If only he'd told the police what he knew sooner. Then he'd probably still be alive.'

Chapter Forty-Seven

LOTTIE STRUGGLED to eat much breakfast the following morning. A second person was dead and Tilly had been dismissed from her job. The return to Fortescue Manor hadn't been as fun as she'd anticipated.

Lord Buckley-Phipps entered the room and inspected the breakfast laid out on the sideboard.

'Good morning, Ivan,' said Mrs Moore. Her mood was glum.

'Good morning, Roberta. Now don't look so disheartened. The Yard are sending their best detective today. He's due to arrive at Shrewsbury railway station at midday. He'll get to the bottom of this in no time.'

'I hope so.'

Mr Duxbury entered the room, greeted Lord Buckley-Phipps, and addressed Lottie. 'Detective Inspector Lloyd would like to see you in the music room, Miss Sprigg.'

'Me?'

'He's finally realised he needs your help, Lottie!' said Mrs Moore. 'Perhaps you can solve this before the detective from the Yard gets here.'

. . .

Lottie made her way to the music room with Rosie. She didn't feel confident the detective would ask for her help. He didn't seem the sort.

'Miss Sprigg. Please sit down.'

Detective Inspector Lloyd puffed on his pipe. In the centre of the table sat a sackcloth bag.

'What's that?' asked Lottie.

'You tell me.'

'I've never seen it before.'

He laughed. 'You're a good actress, Miss Sprigg.'

'It's the truth!'

'Then what was it doing under your bed?'

'Under my bed?'

'An anonymous note was delivered to the station late last night.'

'Saying what?'

'It had two words written on it. "Lottie Sprigg".'

'Really?'

'While you were at breakfast, I asked permission from the housekeeper to check your room. She accompanied me and we found this bag.'

'What's in it?'

'Surely you know what's in it?'

'I don't.'

'Why don't you look inside?'

Lottie opened out the top of the bag and pulled out two items. A pair of rusty cutters and a piece of thin cable.

Lottie gasped. 'I've never seen these things before!'

The detective sat back in his chair. 'So you're denying all knowledge of them?'

'Of course!'

'Which is just what I would expect the murderer to do.'

'Yes, the murderer would deny it. And so would an innocent person! I can't think of any reason why these things
would be in my room. Someone must have put them there to
get me into trouble.'

'Do you ever lock your door, Miss Sprigg?'

'No. I didn't think there was a need to. But I will from
now on. Someone clearly has it in for me. Have you dusted
these items for fingerprints?'

'Yes, but they've both been wiped clean.'

'So if the cutters belonged to me and I'd hidden them
under my bed, presumably I was hoping no one would find
them?'

'Yes, I would assume so.'

'So why would I have bothered to wipe my fingerprints off
the cutters if I was assuming no one would look in my room
and find them? Surely I would have been better off discarding
the cutters? Perhaps I could have thrown them into the lake?
They would have sunk to the bottom without a trace and not
incriminated me at all.'

Detective Inspector Lloyd gave a sniff as he considered
this.

'And why would I have hidden a section of brake cable in
my room? Surely I would have wanted to be rid of that too?'
Lottie eyed the rusty cutters. 'Those don't even look sharp
enough to cut through the cable.'

She picked up the cutters and the piece of cable and
attempted it. The cutters bent the cable but didn't cut
through it.

'I knew it!' she said. 'These cutters are far too blunt to do
anything! I don't think these were the cutters which were used
to cut Tom's brake cables.'

'Let me try,' said Detective Lloyd. Lottie handed the
items to him and watched as he attempted to cut the cable
in two. His knuckles turned white as he gripped the handles

185

of the cutters as hard as possible. But the cable remained intact.

'See?' said Lottie. 'Someone's rummaged around in the tool shed and put these things in my room in the hope I'll be arrested.'

The detective placed the cutters and cable back on the table and scratched his temple. 'I suppose that could be a possibility,' he said.

'You *suppose*? I think it's quite obvious that's what has happened!'

Chapter Forty-Eight

LOTTIE STORMED out of the music room. Not only had someone gone to the trouble of trying to frame her, but the hapless detective had fallen for it!

This could only be Harry's work.

She headed for the service staircase with Rosie in tow. She found Harry in the servants' hall reading a copy of the *Sporting Times*.

'Busy?' she said.

'I'm having a quick break.'

'I suppose you think your little stunt was funny,' she snapped.

'My little stunt?' He put the paper down. 'What are you talking about?'

'You know what.'

'No, I don't.'

'You hid some cutters and a cable beneath my bed and sent a note to Detective Inspector Lloyd with my name on.'

Harry's jaw dropped. 'Someone did that?'

'Yes. And I think it was you.'

'I wish I could take credit for it,' he said. 'But it wasn't me. Why would I do something like that?'

'Because you've got something to hide. Perhaps you're the murderer.'

'Now, just a moment...'

'Whatever you've been doing at Clarendon Park, Percy Abercromby must have found out about it.'

'No, he didn't.'

'I think he found out and threatened to tell his father. And what about Daisy?'

Harry's face paled. 'What about her?'

'You were very upset when she went off with Percy Abercromby, weren't you?'

'That's none of your business!'

'You had two reasons to want Percy Abercromby dead. He found out what you were up to and he stole Daisy from you. And there's Tom Granger too! He knew the identity of the culprit. He knew you were the killer and that's why you murdered him.'

'No!' He got to his feet. 'You're quite mistaken!'

'So tell me the truth! I know you were there at Clarendon Park, I saw you.'

'So it *was* you. I was right. You followed me and you had no right to do so. You trespassed.'

'We both did.'

'If you say so. But I'm certain Percy Abercromby had no idea what we were doing there.'

'So you admit you've been doing something?'

'Yes.' He sank back into his chair. 'And Smithy tells me that Lord Abercromby has just found out about it. So I'm going to get into trouble now.'

'How has he found out?'

'Some chap called William Treves got angry with us

because he said we owed him money. According to Smithy, he's told Lord Abercromby about us.'

'Smithy?'

'Stephen Smith. He's a stableboy at Clarendon Park.'

Lottie sat down. 'So you had nothing to do with Percy Abercromby's murder?'

'No! And neither did I cut Tom's brake cables and try to frame you for it. What sort of person does that?'

'A cold-hearted killer.'

'Exactly. It makes our activities seem quite harmless.'

'And what are your activities?'

'Well, seeing as Lord Abercromby has found out, I may as well tell you. I've set myself up as a bookmaker.'

'How do you manage that?'

'I've got a friend who works at Ludlow racecourse. He tells me the odds. And I do my research too.'

'From the *Sporting Times*?'

'Yes.' He glanced at the folded paper in his hands. 'And in the evenings, people know they can find me and Smithy at Clarendon Park stables. It's not easy running it without getting found out. I can't use the telephone because Mr Duxbury or Mrs Hudson will see me doing it. And although Smithy and I exchange some messages and telegrams, there's a danger they'd get found and read. So we have to communicate in other ways. That's what I was doing in the dining room at the time Percy Abercromby was murdered. I was sending a message to Smithy.'

'How?'

'Morse code. With a torch at the window.'

'Really?'

'Smithy starts earlier than me and finishes earlier. So we arranged for Smithy to wait outside beneath the oak tree and watch the dining room windows.'

This made sense to Lottie. The dining room windows

were next to the main entrance. If someone stood in the front garden, they would be able to see the light at the window.

'So that night, I messaged the latest odds to Smithy so he could get to the stables. We had arranged to meet there later that evening, but I couldn't because of the murder. I was halfway through sending the message to Smithy when I heard the dowager call out for help. I knew I couldn't ignore her, I had to go. And she was only in the room next door. And it was while I was helping her up from the floor that I glanced through the library door and saw Percy Abercromby lying there. I didn't realise it was him to begin with, he just looked like a bundle of cloth. Then I went into the room and... that's when I saw him.'

'So, did you see or hear the murderer bump into the dowager?'

'No, I was too busy sending the message to Smithy.'

'If Smithy was standing beneath the oak tree at the front, he must have seen the murderer run out.'

'He says he didn't see him. He must have been too busy writing down the message I was signalling to him. That evening was ruined for us because we weren't able to take bets for the races at Ludlow the next day. Our regular punters weren't happy.'

'Smithy must have been the man who Barty saw beneath the oak tree.'

'Yes, it must have been him.'

'So is it Smithy who's been seen in the gardens?'

'No! I've no idea who that is.'

'So Smithy and that man are two different people.'

'Who's the other man?'

'I wish I knew.' Lottie turned to leave, then decided to ask another question. 'Why did you refuse to serve me at the dinner on the night Percy died?'

'I didn't think you deserved to be there. You were a maid

when you were last here. And, as far as I'm concerned, you still are. I can't believe you're now dining with the lords and ladies. You're no better than me, you know.'

'I don't claim to be. But I do know that Daisy Harris broke your heart. And if you murdered Percy Abercromby in revenge, I shall find the evidence.'

LOTTIE LEFT THE SERVANTS' hall and climbed the service staircase. 'So Harry denies murder and putting the cutters and cable in my room,' she said to Rosie. 'If he's telling the truth, who's responsible?'

She walked through the saloon and made her way to the library. A clock ticked quietly on the mantelpiece as she glanced around the room. What had happened here on that fateful night? Where had the murderer hidden so they could creep up on Percy Abercromby and plunge the knife into his back?

'Hello Lottie.'

Mildred stood in the doorway with a feather duster in her hand.

'Hello Mildred, how are you this morning?'

'I feel sad for Tilly. Tom's death was a big shock for her. And she's lost her job. I know she shouldn't have been stealing, but she only did it for him.'

Rosie gave a small bark. Lottie glanced at her. The dog was lying on the carpet, facing a mahogany cabinet. 'Shush Rosie, we're trying to talk.' She turned back to Mildred. 'You were right about Tilly, though. And I don't think she was cut out for being a maid, was she? Perhaps she'll get a job at the biscuit factory.'

'I hope so.'

Rosie gave another small bark.

'What is it?' said Lottie. 'That's the sort of noise you make when your ball has rolled to a place you can't fetch it from.'

'Perhaps there's a ball under the cabinet?' said Mildred.

'I suppose there must be something under there. She's staring at it intently, isn't she?'

Lottie dropped to her knees and looked beneath. 'I can see a balled-up piece of paper,' she said. 'Perhaps it's another letter which Mrs Moore has thrown away.' She pushed her arm beneath the cabinet but couldn't quite reach it.

'I'll flick it out with my feather duster,' said Mildred. She knelt down and pushed the duster beneath the cabinet, then she pushed out the piece of paper. It rolled out, and Lottie picked it up.

'Hello!' said Barty, striding into the room. 'What have you got there?'

'A ball of paper.' Lottie began to open it out. It looked like a page from a book.

'Put it in the wastepaper basket and fetch your walking shoes, Lottie. Auntie and I are going for a stroll. Come with us!'

Lottie pushed the paper into her skirt pocket and got to her feet. 'I don't have any walking shoes.'

'Why not?'

'I'll explain another time.'

Chapter Fifty

'I CAN'T BELIEVE someone put a pair of cutters and some cable beneath your bed, Lottie,' said Mrs Moore as they strolled towards the rose garden.

'Very sinister,' said Barty. 'It's just as well the Scotland Yard detective will be arriving soon.'

'I wouldn't be so certain about him solving it quickly,' said Mrs Moore. 'It will take him a few days to gather all the information. And I expect we'll all have to be interviewed again.'

'Oh no!' said Barty. 'I'm going to be suspected all over again, aren't I? Just because of that stupid row with Percy. Wait a moment! There's that fellow again!'

Lottie looked in the direction he was pointing and saw a figure in a dark suit.

'Oh, good golly!' cried out Mrs Moore. She flung her lorgnette to her eyes to get a closer look, and Barty took off after the man.

'Barty, be careful!' she cried out.

Lottie watched as Barty sprinted along the path which led to the grotto. The man was already out of sight. 'Do you think he'll catch him?'

'I hope not! He could be attacked!'

Lottie peered down the slope, but Barty had also vanished.

'Oh, what can we do?' said Mrs Moore. 'Back to the house. Quick, Lottie. We need to tell the police!'

Chapter Fifty-One

'OH, I hope Barty will be alright!' said Lady Buckley-Phipps in the drawing room. 'It was very brave of him to go off after the man like that.'

'It was very foolish!' said her husband, pacing the floor. 'He might be armed!'

'Oh, I hope not.'

'It was brave of Barty,' said the dowager. 'A little too brave. I hope he doesn't come to any harm! I couldn't bear it!'

'I hope Barty's alright too,' said Mrs Moore. 'The man he chased is clearly a coward if he runs off at the first sight of someone.'

The drawing room door swung open and Detective Inspector Lloyd marched in with a constable and a handcuffed man. He was lean with thinning dark hair and wore a dark blue suit.

Barty walked in after them, grinning. 'I caught him!' he said.

'Well done, son!' said Lord Buckley-Phipps.

'That's the man!' said the dowager. 'He's the one I saw!'

'That's good to hear, my lady,' said the detective. He

turned to the man and grabbed his collar. 'Why have you been loitering in the gardens?'

'I, I, I was just passing,' stammered the man.

Lottie thought he looked rather pathetic. There was no menace to him at all.

'You can't have been *just passing*. You were found on private property. You were trespassing and snooping. Planning another murder, were you?'

'Murder? No!'

'First Percy Abercromby, then Tom Granger, the delivery boy. Who were you planning to murder next?'

'No one!'

'Come on, tell us! Who's next?'

'I'm not a murderer!'

'Tell us your name!'

'Bertrand Sykes.'

Lottie turned to Mrs Moore, who was shaking her head in dismay.

'And I'm an innocent man,' he added.

'No, you're not!' said Mrs Moore. 'You're a pest.'

The detective turned to her. 'You know this man, Mrs Moore?'

'I've met him a few times in the past.'

'He's a friend of yours, Roberta?' asked Lady Buckley-Phipps.

'Absolutely not. But I met him at a party in London some time ago. His sister lives close by.'

'You didn't reply to my letters, Roberta!' said Mr Sykes.

'I'm Mrs Moore to you. And I didn't reply to your letters because you're only interested in me because of my wealth.'

'Not true, Roberta!'

'Mrs Moore.'

'Not true, Mrs Moore. I would still adore you, even if you were as poor as a church mouse.'

'Detective Inspector Lloyd, can you remove this man from our home please,' said Lady Buckley-Phipps. 'We've established his identity, and he's clearly a nuisance.'

'With pleasure, my lady. I just wanted everyone to get a good look at him because he matches the description of the man who has been seen in the grounds of this home.'

'I only wanted to speak with Mrs Moore,' said Mr Sykes.

'So you admit to loitering in the gardens now?'

'Yes.'

'How many times?'

'I don't know. Most days. But I'm not a murderer!'

'Why did you want to speak to me, Mr Sykes?' asked Mrs Moore.

'You didn't reply to my letters, so I thought I'd come and see you.'

'But you ran away from me!'

He grew bashful. 'I was caught off-guard at that moment. I was embarrassed to have been found hiding behind a tree, I had wanted to plan our encounter better so... I ran.'

Mrs Moore gave a disparaging sigh.

'We'll talk about it more down at the station,' said the detective. 'Take him out please, Constable.' The detective turned back to Lady Buckley-Phipps. 'I do apologise for the disturbance, my lady.'

'Is it him?'

'Is it who?'

'Is it the murderer you've got there?'

'I sincerely hope so. We'll see what he has to say for himself and then have a look at the evidence and alibis and so on. I shall keep you informed, my lady.'

He followed Mr Sykes and the constable out of the room.

'Oh, how embarrassing,' said Mrs Moore. 'I should have replied to his first letter and asked him not to bother me.'

'You can't blame yourself, Roberta,' said Lucinda. 'He's clearly rather strange.'

'But could he be the murderer?' said Barty. 'He doesn't look like one to me.'

'Well, I think he could be the man who knocked me over in the saloon,' said the dowager. 'And he's certainly the one we've seen loitering in the grounds.'

'He says he was here to see Auntie.'

'That could be just an excuse he's using, couldn't it?'

'Bertrand Sykes is an annoyance,' said Mrs Moore. 'And it was clearly him hanging about in the gardens. Although he's odd, I don't see why he would murder Percy Abercromby and Tom Granger.'

'Hopefully all will become clear,' said Lord Buckley-Phipps. 'It's difficult to guess the motivations of an oddball like him.'

'I don't know how he found out I was here,' said Mrs Moore. 'I suppose word gets around.'

'All it takes is for one of the servants to mention it to someone in the village, and soon everybody knows,' said Lady Buckley-Phipps. 'Whatever the man is guilty of, he's been apprehended now and we needn't worry about him anymore.'

As they discussed Mr Sykes, Lottie remembered the balled-up page she'd shoved into her pocket. She took it out again and smoothed it out on her lap. Then she began reading the dense text. It wasn't long before she realised which book the page was from. She got to her feet and slipped out of the room to return to the library. Rosie followed at her heels.

Chapter Fifty-Two

'OH, THERE YOU ARE, LOTTIE,' said Mrs Moore as she arrived in the library. 'I was wondering where you'd got to. The detective from Scotland Yard has arrived, and he wants to speak to everyone in the drawing room.' She rolled her eyes. 'I can't believe we're having to go over everything again. It's becoming quite tedious.'

'I hope he's the sort of detective who listens to other people's ideas,' said Lottie.

'Do you have some ideas?'

'Yes.'

'And you've got a book with you.'

'That's right.' Lottie glanced down at it. 'I think it could be evidence.'

Detective Inspector Hanbury was a thin man with a thick moustache and spectacles.

'Is everyone here?' he asked as he opened his notebook.

'We think so,' said Lord Buckley-Phipps. 'Do you want the servants here as well?'

'I'll speak to them separately downstairs,' said the detective. 'Now then, I only have some cursory knowledge of this case, so let's start at the very beginning, shall we?'

Lottie felt her shoulders slump. She couldn't face more hours of discussing the same information. Would it be rude to interrupt him?

'I need the names of everyone who attended the dinner that night,' said the detective.

'Excuse me, sir.' Lottie put her hand up. 'But I think I know who committed these crimes.'

'Do you?' Light reflected on the detective's spectacles as he turned to her. 'Who are you?'

'Miss Lottie Sprigg.'

'And you know who did this?'

'Yes. I think so.'

'You think so?'

'But I don't think people will be happy with me when I suggest the name.'

'Well, I'm assuming you have a reason for suggesting the name?'

'Yes.'

'If there's a good reason for suspecting the person, then I don't think people can argue with it too much. Who do you think did it?'

Lottie got to her feet and took in a breath. 'I think the Dowager Lady Buckley-Phipps is responsible.'

Chapter Fifty-Three

'WHAT?' Lord Buckley-Phipps jumped to his feet. 'My elderly mother? You take back that accusation at once! How dare you! Who do you think you are? You need to remember your place, young lady. You can't accuse my mother of something so despicable!'

'Are you sure you're right, Lottie?' asked Mrs Moore. 'It would be a terrible mistake to accuse her ladyship.'

Lottie took in another breath. 'I wish it was a mistake. But I don't think it is.'

'Not Granny.' Barty shook his head. 'Absolutely not.'

'Well, if this young lady is making an accusation, she needs a reason for it,' said Detective Inspector Hanbury. 'Let's hear her out.'

Lottie swallowed, aware of the hostile mood in the room. She could feel the dowager's eyes on her but she avoided her gaze. 'I don't think the Dowager Lady-Buckley Phipps wanted to mend the feud with the Abercrombys. During the dinner on that fateful night, she told me she was loyal to her husband even after his death. I know her late husband would have disagreed with mending the feud because Lord Buckley-Phipps said so.'

'That's right, I did,' said Lord Buckley-Phipps. 'My father would never have agreed to the dinner and making friends with the Abercrombys. It makes sense that Mother didn't agree with it either, but she remained tactfully quiet on the matter for Lucinda's sake. And this certainly doesn't mean my mother murdered Percy Abercromby!'

'During the dinner, the dowager also remarked that Percy Abercromby was the family's only son,' said Lottie. 'She wondered what would become of the Clarendon Park estate if something happened to him. I realised then that someone wishing to harm the Abercromby family would probably choose Percy as their target.'

'But not my mother!' said Lord Buckley-Phipps.

'So far, there is no evidence,' said the detective. 'Have you anything else, Miss Sprigg?'

'Yes. A few hours ago, I found a balled-up piece of paper under a cabinet in the library,' she said. 'Actually, my dog Rosie found it. She thought it was something she could play with. I have it here.' She pulled it out of her pocket. 'It's a page from a book and, from what I can tell, it appears to be an account of the Battle of Naseby. My history knowledge isn't great, but I'm sure that was a famous battle during the English Civil War.'

'Yes, I believe it was,' said the detective. 'How is this relevant, Miss Sprigg?'

'I shall explain. As you can see, the page has been torn from the book.' She held it up so everyone could see.

'Has it come from one of the volumes about the English Civil War in the library?' said Lord Buckley-Phipps.

'Yes.'

'Those volumes are extremely precious! And someone just

ripped a page out from one of them? Pure vandalism! It's enough to make my father turn in his grave!'

'I recall you invited Percy Abercromby to look at the books about the Civil War after dinner, my lord,' said Lottie.

'I did.'

'And you asked Barty to show Mr Abercromby the books.'

'Yes.'

'I didn't rip the page out!' said Barty. 'In fact, Percy didn't even look at the books while I was in there. He was too busy shouting at me! Obviously I didn't stand for it for long and left before I completely lost my cool.'

'I can only imagine that Percy Abercromby took one of the books from the shelf after you left, Barty,' said Lottie.

'Yes, he must have done. He shouted at me, then calmed himself down by reading about something very dull.'

'I had a look in the library for the book which the page had come from,' said Lottie. 'And as I looked at the volumes for the English Civil War, I noticed that one of them was out of place. Volume seven was between volumes nine and ten. I wondered if volume seven was the one which had been looked at most recently. I looked through it and found that it contained an account of the Battle of Naseby. And it didn't take me long to find where the page had been torn out.'

'But what does this prove?' said Lady Buckley-Phipps.

'I think the book was the one which Percy Abercromby was reading when he was attacked,' said Lottie. 'His assailant must have approached him from behind as he stood by the bookcase reading. He would have collapsed to the floor when he was attacked and dropped the book. I think the murderer quickly put the book back on the shelf before they fled. That's why it had not been put back in its proper place.'

'I can't believe no one noticed that earlier,' said the detective. 'But why did the murderer bother to put the book back on the shelf? Why not just leave it on the floor next to Mr Abercromby?'

'Because the book was damaged,' said Lottie. 'And I think the murderer wished to disguise that fact.'

'Why?'

'Because if you have a look at the book, it's quite clearly been damaged by a dog.'

'How?'

'There are claw marks inside where the page was ripped out, and there are tooth marks in the cover where the book must have been in a dog's jaws.'

'But this could have happened at any time!' said Lord Buckley-Phipps.

'If it had, then I think the owner of the dog would have told someone about it so the book could be repaired,' said Lottie. 'The dog's owner tried to cover up what had happened because it happened at the same time Percy Abercromby was murdered. I believe that once he dropped the book he was reading, it landed on the floor open at the account of the Battle of Naseby. I think one of the Dowager Lady Buckley-Phipps' dogs then approached the book and pawed at it, ripping out a page and damaging the other pages with its claws. And while the Dowager Lady Buckley-Phipps was wiping the handle of the dagger free of fingerprints, one of her dogs began chewing the book. As soon as she noticed this, she presumably had to wrestle the book from the dog's jaws and put it back on the shelf. She was no doubt desperate to get out of the library, so she quickly replaced the book with the other volumes. She presumably had no time to check it was in its right place. As she was leaving the library, she must have noticed the ripped out page on the floor. I think she must have screwed it into a ball and kicked it beneath the cabinet so no one would see it. Then, as soon as she was in the saloon, she fell to the floor and cried for help. That's when she claimed the murderer had knocked her over.'

'Ludicrous! My mother would never do such a thing!' said Lord Buckley-Phipps.

'But what about the man I saw standing beneath the oak tree?' said Barty. 'Who was he?'

'Stephen Smith,' said Lottie. 'An acquaintance of Harry Lewis. He was standing there because Harry was flashing him a coded message by torch from the dining room windows.'

'What?'

'The pair were running an illegal bookmakers and Harry was messaging him the latest odds.'

'Good grief.'

'An illegal bookmakers?' said Lord Buckley-Phipps. 'Under my roof?'

'Mainly in Lord Abercromby's stable block,' said Lottie. 'But he's aware of it now. I spoke to Harry and he told me Stephen Smith didn't see a man running out of the main entrance while he was waiting under the oak tree. According to her ladyship, she was knocked over by the murderer who then ran outside. When I heard Stephen Smith hadn't seen him, I wondered if I should doubt her ladyship's version of events.'

'Very interesting indeed,' said Detective Inspector Hanbury. 'I would like to see the book.'

'I have it here,' said Lottie. She passed it to him and the room was silent as the detective examined the bite marks on the book. 'This certainly looks like the work of a dog,' he said.

'The missing page is number three hundred and forty-seven,' said Lottie.

The detective found the place in the book and examined the damage which had been done to it.

'So what's the verdict, Detective?' asked Lord Buckley-Phipps.

'This book requires some detailed examination, but from what I can see of the damage, I concur with Miss Sprigg. A dog has indeed attacked this book.'

'But Miss Sprigg could have fabricated this evidence!' said Lord Buckley-Phipps. 'She could have ripped the page out herself and encouraged her dog to chew the book!'

'But why would Lottie wish to do that?' said Mrs Moore. 'Nobody wants to believe that her ladyship could be capable of such an act, but Lottie has uncovered evidence which is rather damning. There's no one else in this household who owns dogs which chew everything they can get their paws on.'

'Lottie has a dog.'

'Yes, but Rosie doesn't chew things like her ladyship's dogs do. In fact, I've never seen her chew anything which she shouldn't.'

'What about Tom Granger, Miss Sprigg?' asked the detective. 'Why was he murdered?'

'I think he somehow knew the Dowager Lady Buckley-Phipps was the culprit,' said Lottie. 'Perhaps he saw her at the crime scene? I'm not sure. But I think her ladyship's sharp rose cutters would have snipped through the brake cables on his bicycle quite easily.'

'Scandalous!' said Lord Buckley-Phipps. 'What an accusation!' He turned to the dowager. 'What do you say about this, Mother? I think it's an outrage! A young woman who was once a maid in this house. A maid who served us for *five years* and someone we *trusted* is now accusing the most respected member of the Buckley-Phipps family of murder!'

The dowager gave a sigh. 'I say she's a very clever young woman indeed.'

Chapter Fifty-Four

'ARE you not going to deny it, Mother?' asked Lord Buckley-Phipps.

'What's the point, Ivan? Lottie's worked it all out. And I'm too old and tired to be carrying on with any more lies.'

'So you *did* do it?'

'No!' gasped Lady Buckley-Phipps.

'Granny!' cried out Barty. 'Please tell me it's not true!'

'I wish I could, Barty dear. I'm not setting a very good example to you, am I? But I'm afraid I did stick Ivan's letter opener into Percy's back and I don't regret it at all.'

'No, Mother! It can't be true. Come now, you're not thinking straight. You need to have a lie down for a while and then you'll come to your senses, I feel sure of it.'

'I don't need a lie down, Ivan. I'm quite alright.'

'But why did you do it, my lady?' asked Lady Buckley-Phipps.

'Because Percy Abercromby was an irksome little toe-rag. I've never liked the Abercromby family and I never will. But as Abercrombys go, he was the very worst of them! He would have been an absolute thorn in your side, Barty.'

'I could have handled him Granny, there was no need for you to murder him!'

'It was time for the Abercromby line to come to an end.'

'You can't decree such things, Granny!'

'Why can't I? Great families in this country have historically done such things.'

'But this is the twentieth century, Granny! Things are different now.'

The dowager tutted. 'So I keep being reminded. But I realised that if Percy Abercromby was no longer around, then Clarendon Park would pass to a distant relative of Lord and Lady Abercromby. Once Lord Abercromby has died, the estate will go to someone obscure. They won't care about us and we won't care about them. Not only will the feud end, but we will also have won it!'

'*Won*, Mother? This has never been about winning anything!'

'In my book it has. The Abercrombys have been vanquished by the Buckley-Phipps family.'

Lord Buckley-Phipps shook his head into dismay. 'You can't just take these matters into your own hands.'

'Well I'm afraid I did, Ivan. And perhaps I would have spared Percy Abercromby if he had been a nicer person. Unfortunately, he had no respect for other people and he had even less respect for animals!'

'Animals?' said Barty.

'Dogs in particular.'

'Not everyone likes dogs, Granny.'

'No, I realise that. Some dogs are an acquired taste, especially mine. I love my dogs, but I don't expect other people to share my enthusiasm for them. I do expect people to treat them respectfully, though.'

'Mother, what have your dogs got to do with this?'

'I'm in the middle of explaining why Percy Abercromby was such a deplorable human being.'

'I think it's fair to say none of us warmed to him. But was he really that bad?'

'I saw him when he didn't know I was there, Ivan.'

'When?'

'Before dinner that evening. I saw him kick Lord Byron.'

'No! Badly?'

'Not very badly. But it was a kick. I was just going downstairs for dinner and I'm a little slow on the stairs. The dogs went ahead of me, like they usually do, so they were milling about at the foot of the stairs. I was still quite a way up when I saw Percy pass by the bottom of the stairs on his way to the smoking room. My dogs are quite inquisitive, as you know, so they gave his legs a few sniffs.'

'Did they bark at him?' asked Lord Buckley-Phipps.

'A little. But no more than usual. And Lord Byron...' The dowager tailed off as emotion consumed her. She rested her hand on her chest and composed herself. 'Lord Byron happened to stroll in front of him and that Percy jabbed at him with his foot. Poor Lord Byron gave a little yelp, and I was so horrified that I was simply frozen still on the stairs. I couldn't believe what I'd seen! He jabbed at the little dog with his foot and went on his way without a care in the world!'

'Poor Lord Byron!' said Lady Buckley-Phipps. 'Is he alright?'

'He's fine. But I didn't know that at the time. I couldn't get down those stairs quickly enough. I almost tripped and fell! And if that had happened, and I'd injured myself, then I shouldn't think Percy Abercromby could have cared a jot! I picked up Lord Byron and fortunately there wasn't a mark on him. He was quite happy and licked my cheek, as he always does. So that was a relief. But it was deeply upsetting to see him treated in that way. I was ready to march into the smoking room there and then and confront the young man. I was incensed! But I told myself that revenge is a dish best served cold. So that's when I went off to the study to fetch the letter opener from your drawer, Ivan.'

'What made you think of the letter opener?'

'I'd seen it on your desk plenty of times over the years and it always struck me what a subtle yet useful weapon it was. And so easy to keep in a handbag too. And then, at dinner, when plans were made for Percy to visit the library afterwards, I decided I could visit the library too. I loitered in the gardens near the library while I waited for Percy to finish shouting at Barty. What a horrible young man! Fancy carrying on at my grandson in that way!'

'I saw you through the library windows, Granny,' said Barty. 'I just assumed you were walking your dogs.'

'I was.'

'I had no idea you were planning to go into the library and finish off Percy Abercromby. If I'd known, I would have stopped you!'

'Why?'

'Because look at how much trouble you're in now!'

'But it was all worth it, Barty. The Buckley-Phipps family has won. Just think how proud your grandfather would have been.'

'So you say you were loitering outside the library, my lady,' said the detective. 'Then what happened?'

'I saw Barty marching out of the main entrance. But he didn't see me because he turned left in the direction of the deer park. And then I saw that awful Abercromby boy open the library door and shout after Barty. What a disgrace. Fancy being invited as a guest to someone's home and then yelling like a stallholder at Lowton Chorley market! A disgraceful young man. He pulled the library door shut. But if you know that door well, you know you have to close it in a certain way otherwise it stays off the latch. It was very easy to silently open that door and creep up on him.

'He was standing by the bookcase and had just pulled out one of those war books. I leant my stick against a chair and crept towards him. I can be very stealthy when I need to be. Not so the dogs. They came in with me and, I'm afraid to say, they yapped at him again. He turned and saw me and barely acknowledged me. Another example of the young man's rudeness! He was too busy reading about the Battle of Naseby to make polite conversation. So he turned to look at me, muttered a hello and then turned back to his book. His back was turned to me. And that was his fatal mistake. I took the dagger out of my handbag.'

'That's when you stabbed him in the back?' asked Lord Buckley-Phipps.

'I'm afraid so. I did it for this family and I did it for my dog. And when he toppled over, I felt rather pleased about it. I also realised I'd done something terrible. And that's when panic set in. I knew I had to get out of there as quickly as possible. Anyone could have found me there! But then I saw what Wordsworth had done to the book. I know those volumes were extremely important to my late husband. I didn't care for them myself, but he did. And I knew Ivan would be upset if he saw one of them was damaged. So I had to return it to the shelf. There wasn't time to put on my reading glasses and check I'd put it in exactly the right place. And Miss Sprigg is quite right, it was only when I'd put the book back on the shelf when I noticed that page on the floor. If the fire had been lit in the library, then I would have thrown the page into it. But it wasn't, and I didn't want someone finding it there. So I screwed it up and knocked it under the cabinet with my walking stick. My mistake was not disposing of it properly.

'As soon as I was out of the library, I fell to the floor

because I needed people to believe I was a victim. And I made up the fleeing murderer because I knew he would become a distraction.'

'And it worked, Mother!' said Lord Buckley-Phipps. 'We all believed you!'

'All of you apart from Miss Sprigg. I can't believe I didn't destroy that page. And you found it, Miss Sprigg.'

'My dog found it.'

'Even so, your powers of deduction are very good indeed.'

Detective Inspector Hanbury scratched his head. 'So you're admitting to the murder of Mr Percy Abercromby, Dowager Lady Buckley-Phipps?'

'I'm afraid I am. I'm not proud of it, and I acted impulsively. But what's done is done, and he was a nasty piece of work.'

'And what about Tom Granger?' asked the detective.

'Oh yes, I suppose there's him as well. Well, he was stealing from the house.'

'Stealing? Why didn't you report him?'

'Because he saw me loitering by the library. I feared that if I reported him, then he would report me.'

'How did you know he was stealing?'

'Because I saw him in the dining room a few days ago. I asked him what he was doing there, and he said he'd just made a delivery. He'd presumably reached the dining room via the service stairs close by. But I've never seen a delivery boy in the dining room before and I feared he may have taken some silver. I asked him to empty his pockets, and he did so. He had nothing on him at the time, but I don't know if he'd hidden something somewhere other than his pockets. Who knows? I was about to ring the dining room bell for assistance, and he said that he'd seen me by the library on the night of Percy Abercromby's murder. I recalled seeing him cycle past while I was loitering there and I didn't think a mere delivery boy would have noticed any relevance to me being there. But he'd worked it out and I couldn't risk him telling someone what he'd seen.'

'So you cut the brake cables on his bicycle, Granny?' said Barty.

'Yes, Miss Sprigg was right again. I ensure my rose clipping shears are kept nice and sharp.'

'Did you put the cutters and cable in my room, my lady?' said Lottie.

'Yes. I found them in the woodshed and put the bag under your bed while you were out somewhere. Young Tilly saw me up in the attics, but I swore her to secrecy. If there was anyone I had to worry about then it was you, Lottie. I'd heard all about your sleuthing skills while you were travelling with Mrs Moore. I had to do my best to get you into trouble. I suppose it was a clumsy attempt, but Detective Inspector Lloyd seemed to fall for it.'

'You tried to frame Lottie?' said Mrs Moore.

'I had to. I couldn't have anyone suspecting me. And I should be grateful to Mr Sykes, he chose to loiter about in the gardens and became a suspect! That was very useful for a while.'

Lord Buckley-Phipps shook his head. 'I never would have imagined it,' he said. 'My own mother. How on earth are we going to explain this to Lord and Lady Abercromby?'

'We don't have to explain anything,' said Lady Buckley-Phipps. 'Detective Inspector Hanbury can tell them, and we shall keep a dignified silence. It was nice to make their acquaintance for a few hours, but I can't see there ever being any friendship between the two families after this. The feud is destined to last for another few centuries at least.'

Chapter Fifty-Five

LOTTIE WALKED in the gardens with Rosie and Mrs Moore the following day.

'I really thought you'd got it wrong when you said the dowager was a suspect,' said Mrs Moore. 'I don't think any of us could have imagined her doing such a thing. It was incredibly brave of you to name her.'

'It wasn't brave,' said Lottie. 'The evidence pointed to her.'

'Well, between you and me,' Mrs Moore lowered her voice, 'Lucinda has never liked her mother-in-law very much. Now she no longer has to be so polite about her. Poor Ivan's very upset though. As is Barty. Any hopes he had of a friendship with Evelyn Abercromby have probably been dashed by the fact his grandmother murdered her brother. It's a shame the family feud won't ever be mended now. Oh look, here comes Barty.'

The young man strode towards them with three Jack Russell dogs scampering ahead of him. They ran up to Rosie and sniffed her. She moved a little this time, cautiously sniffing Wordsworth.

'How are you, Barty?'

'I'm holding up. Thank you, Auntie. It's impressive how these three little dogs can lift one's spirits. Although it's Wordsworth's fault Granny was arrested for murder. If he hadn't attacked that old war book, then she would probably have got away with it.'

'I think she would have,' said Mrs Moore. 'And we'd all still be assuming Mr Sykes did it.'

'I think all the dogs played an important role in solving the case,' said Lottie. 'It was Rosie who discovered the torn out page beneath the cabinet in the library.'

'So she did!' said Barty. 'What a team of dog detectives. They did far better than Detective Inspector Lloyd, didn't they? Oh look, who's that walking over here?' He shielded his eyes from the sun. 'It looks like Mildred.'

'Lottie!' She gave her a wave. 'There's a lady here to see you,' said the maid as she got closer. 'She says her name is... oh no, I've forgotten it now!' She clasped her hand to her mouth in embarrassment. 'She has an accent. I think she said she was from the orphanage.'

'Miss Beaufort?'

'Yes, that's what she said!'

They walked back to the house together.

'I think you should come and meet Miss Beaufort, Mrs Moore,' said Lottie as they walked into the saloon. Barty went with the dogs to the smoking room and Mildred returned to her work.

'Well, that would be nice. Perhaps she has some amusing stories from your childhood to share?'

'I hope not!'

In the morning room, Lottie introduced Mrs Moore and Miss Beaufort to each other.

'I apologise for calling on you at a difficult time,' said Miss Beaufort. 'I heard about the arrest of the Dowager Lady Buckley-Phipps and I wondered if I should delay my visit. But the truth is, I've delayed it enough already.'

'What do you mean by that?' asked Lottie.

'When you called on us four days ago, I'm afraid Miss Spencer wasn't completely truthful with you.'

'She lied?'

'She merely told you what she tells everybody who asks about their parents. She doesn't believe it's helpful to reunite anyone. In her mind, each child who comes to the orphanage must forget about any family they had. She believes it's too unsettling for children to think about their parents or any other family members.'

'That seems a little unreasonable,' said Mrs Moore.

'I think it's an old-fashioned attitude. Although I can't possibly say that to Miss Spencer.'

'No, I imagine not.'

'Sometimes people visit the orphanage and ask about children there. Sometimes they're parents who left a baby there and want to find out how they got on. They don't necessarily want to see them, they just want to be reassured their child is thriving.'

'They want to hear they made the right decision about leaving them there?' said Mrs Moore.

'Yes, that could be a reason.'

'So when parents call at the orphanage and ask about their children, what do you say?' asked Lottie.

'Miss Spencer tells them all the same thing. That the child is fit and well and has received an education. She also says the child doesn't wish to have anything to do with their family.'

Lottie took in a breath before she spoke. 'So, has anyone ever called in and asked about me? Is that why you're here?'

'Yes, Lottie.' Miss Beaufort smiled. 'Someone called in and asked about you while you were travelling.'

Lottie gasped. 'That recently? Who was it?'

'A lady. She didn't give her name.'

'My mother?'

'I don't know, Lottie. But she gave us the date and time you were left on the doorstep. That's how we knew it was you she was enquiring about. She was able to describe the blanket you were wrapped in too.'

Lottie felt tears at the back of her eyes. 'I think I know already what Miss Spencer said to her.'

Miss Beaufort gave a sad nod.

'I knew it.' Lottie took out her handkerchief and wiped her eyes. Mrs Moore put an arm around her shoulders.

'But this isn't the end of it, Lottie,' said Miss Beaufort. 'I think you can find her.'

'Really? Do you think she wants to be found?'

'Yes I do. And I've heard how good you are at solving mysteries. I think you can solve this one too.'

THE END

* * *

Thank you

Thank you for reading *Murder in the Library*. I really hope you enjoyed it! Here are a few ways to stay in touch:

- Join my mailing list and receive a FREE short story *Murder at the Castle*: marthabond.com/murder-at-the-castle
- Like my brand new Facebook page: facebook.com/marthabondauthor

A free Lottie Sprigg mystery

Find out what happens when Lottie, Rosie and Mrs Moore visit Scotland in this free mystery _Murder at the Castle_!

When Lottie Sprigg accompanies her employer to New Year celebrations in a Scottish castle, she's excited about her first ever Hogmanay. The guests are in party spirits and enjoying the pipe band, dancing and whisky.

But the mood turns when a guest is found dead in the billiard room. Who committed the crime? With the local police stuck in the snow, Lottie puts her sleuthing skills to the test. She makes good progress until someone takes drastic action to stop her uncovering the truth...

Visit my website to claim your free copy:
    marthabond.com/murder-at-the-castle

Or scan the code on the following page:

Murder in the Grotto

Book 2 in the Lottie Sprigg Country House Mystery Series!

Christmas at Fortescue Manor is always celebrated in style. The highlight is the annual Christmas Fayre hosted by Lord and Lady Buckley-Phipps. With ice skating, entertainment, and tobogganing, Lottie Sprigg and her dog, Rosie, are looking forward to the festivities.

But Lottie's sleuthing skills are called upon when a body is found in the spooky shell grotto in the manor house grounds. Locals have long said the place is cursed. Can Lottie separate fact from fiction and uncover the culprit before they strike again?

Get your copy: mybook.to/murder-grotto

Also by Martha Bond

Lottie Sprigg Country House Mystery Series:

Murder in the Library
Murder in the Grotto

Lottie Sprigg Travels Mystery Series:

Murder in Venice
Murder in Paris
Murder in Cairo
Murder in Monaco
Murder in Vienna

Writing as Emily Organ:

Augusta Peel Mystery Series:

Death in Soho
Murder in the Air
The Bloomsbury Murder

Made in United States
Orlando, FL
15 November 2023

38994282R00139